THE ADVENTURE

Moonrise Mountain
Temple of Night and Wind
The Tournament

Jennifer M Zeiger

Illustrated By
Joseph Apolinar
&
Justin Allen

Published by Jennifer M Zeiger

Printed by Amazon CreateSpace

First Edition: November 30, 2017

Cover Design: Joseph Apolinar

Illustrated by: Joseph Apolinar and Justin Allen

ISBN- 13: 978-1543231236
         10: 1543231233

jenniferzeiger.com
jennifer.m.zeiger@gmail.com

To my husband, Nathan, your constant encouragement means the world to me.

Amazing Wonderful Incredible Kickstarter Backers

Esther Rohman
(author's niece)
Chloe Sebring
Gideon Sebring
Nikita
Teri Clark
Cindy Wittebort
Jael Rohman
The Johnson's
Maggie Becker
Matthew X. Gomez
Sora & Nic Wondra
Emily Steele
Kaydee Glumac
Bonnie Jeanne
Kim Bussey
Bernadette Lyon
The Seibert Kids
Bonnie Walters

Kiani Jackson
Charlie & Krista Stiffler
Chris & Tiffany Austin
Marchand Boyle
Trey & Tyler Stein
A. Zeiger
Jonathan Zeiger
Leslie Rohman
Nick Rohman
Mom and Dad
Shalyn Clark
J.C. Wolfe
Gayle Flentge
Samland Family
Wieney
Doug Clark
Timothy Kuyper
Kurt Cederburg

Contents

<u>Attention</u>

This book is not intended for you to read straight through! Heaven knows, it'll make no sense if you do.

Instead, read until the book gives you a choice on what to do, and then follow the directions to see what happens when you decide. Some decisions will lead to success and fame and others, my poor reader, may lead to misfortune or even death.

Choose wisely, for there be monsters within these seemingly innocent pages.

Best of luck!

The Adventure
of
Moonrise Mountain
By Jennifer M Zeiger

Illustrated by
Joseph Apolinar

 **T**hat morning you left the cabin with a warm cloak slung across your shoulders and a sack full of golden apples in your hand. The day dawned warm for late winter and the cloak was enough for the short trip you had in mind.

At the top of Moonrise Mountain lives a herd of wild horses. The town's people say that if you hold an apple in your hand and stand statue still, a few of the horses might come to you. Some say if you give the horses a few apples, and you're very lucky, they'll let you ride across Moonrise Mountain bareback like the heroes of old.

From what you can learn, however, no one's ever actually approached the herd and received a nibble of horse lips for their preferred apple. Most, in fact, won't even approach the woods at the base of the mountain. It's too dangerous, they say.

Your curiosity about the subject is well known. You've talked with everyone in town and yet, besides the folktale, no one can tell you more. It's time to find out if the stories are true.

The bag of apples swings with your step, their comfortable weight encouraging you along like a pull at your hand. Excitement fills your thoughts and limbs as the snow beneath each step crunches with the crust of age. Your cloak is thrown back on your shoulders because, as the sun rises over your shoulder, the day warms to the point that you don't really need the garment.

Around noon, a chill wind kicks up. It throws drifts of snow into the air, creating little dust devils. The day darkens and you look up to find black clouds obscuring the sun. Those ominous puffs roll in with heavy intent.

Pulling your hood up, you quicken your step toward the woods that surround the foot of Moonrise Mountain. Just as you reach the towering pines, great flakes of wet snow begin swirling to the ground.

A few steps into the trees, you glance back to see the snow has already covered your prints. Even the prints sheltered by the branches are starting to fill in with a layer of fresh white.

Shrugging your cloak snug around your shoulders and clasping it closed under your chin, you shiver anyway. You could go back but the snow's heavy enough you can't see the edge of the trees anymore. Instead you're faced with a wall of moving, shifting, and swirling cold.

You walk farther into the forest with the intention of finding shelter to wait out the storm. The ground gives beneath your feet, and you tumble downward until the sheer depth of snow makes you stop. Before you looms a dark circle, the mouth of a cave that slants into the forest floor.

Considering you were intending to find shelter, this could be a wonderful refuge from the storm. Beyond where you sit, the floor is dry, safely covered by the slant to the cave's opening.

But trolls inhabit the woods. Great snow beasts that love to hide in just such caves. They're the reason most of the town's people won't even approach the woods.

You could scramble back out into the swirling blizzard. Your chances of getting home are slim without getting lost, but your woods instructor, a Mister Shaffer, taught you how to shelter under pine trees for survival. You might even be able to get a small fire going for warmth.

If you brave the cave, go to page 5
If you decide to find a tree, go to page 9

The wind howls at the mouth of the cave with a deep, hollow bellow. The forest beyond is obscured except for the barely discernible towering shapes of trees that appear and disappear in the swirling snow. You tell yourself you'd get lost if you wandered in that mess but, to be totally honest, you're already lost. At least exploring farther into the dark cavern promises a dry place to shelter.

Placing your left hand against the cold stone, you shuffle inside. The cavern floor bites through the soles of your shoes with rocky teeth and you stumble as the bag of apples bumps your leg. You hold the bag steady with your free hand and continue forward. Loose rocks clatter across the floor when your feet encounter them, but you can't see their erratic paths in the total darkness.

"Ouch!" A rock, firmly embedded into the ground, stubs your left big toe. Pain radiates through your foot, but you quickly forget it as light flares to life about ten paces ahead.

A grizzled old hand holds up a torch. With deep apprehension, you follow the hand down a bony arm. Your scrutiny stops at a scraggly beard surrounding a gap-toothed grin.

The old man coughs a laugh.

"Look, Ingrid, you were right," he says. "A snack's stumbled into your cave."

"A snack?" Your brain stumbles over that word.

There's shuffling, and deep shadows loom behind the old man until they resolve into the heavy white-draped shoulders of a snow troll. She's a brute of a beast with a short snout and great fangs drooling saliva down her chin. Her big, intelligent eyes tighten into what might be a smile.

Those eyes look you up and down like you'd be finger-licking good, and you can't get your eyes to look away as a fresh glob of saliva drips down her fangs. She grunts and steps up to stand directly behind the old man. He doesn't seem to notice the drool that drips onto his shoulder.

You shrink against the wall, wishing you'd looked for a weapon before exploring. The mouth of the cave's not far, you might be  able to reach it if you bolt but Ingrid has got long, powerful legs. Plus, it's pitch black beyond the old man's torch and the tunnel you just came down isn't totally straight. You swallow as your mind conjures the image of you smacking into a wall as you try to escape.

You step backward toward the entrance and the bag of apples bumps your knee. Maybe you can offer the old man an apple or two? Considering the troll's looming over him and he's not running in terror, he seems to be friends with the beast. Maybe he can keep Ingrid from eating you if you make friends with him?

If you bolt from the cave, go to page 17
If you offer an apple, go to page 25

Stories of snow trolls with fangs the length of your forearm and razor sharp claws spin through your head. Such stories are common, new ones coming in once or twice a month because the beasts love the forests surrounding Moonrise Mountain. They're not like other trolls. They don't care to cook their meals or spice them before enjoying. They're more simple than that. Snow trolls love the chase directly before they eat. You shudder and head out of the cave, not wanting to risk encountering such a beast.

Cold snow pelts your skin with tiny, biting stings as soon as you step out. With the blinding, swirling curtain of white, you don't stand much of a chance of getting home without getting lost, but if you can find a big pine with low hanging branches, you might be able to get a fire going in the small shelter.

Flip to page 11 to continue.

The cold eats away at you while you consider. Ingrid's quiet now, but you haven't heard her reenter the cave, so you know she's still searching.

The thought of a fire, its warm glow chasing the ice from your limbs, calls to you. You decide it's your best chance to survive the night, but first you have to wait awhile longer to be sure Ingrid's given up.

Wind howls and the weight of snow on top of your cloak grows imperceptibly heavier. A thud sounds nearby. You suck in your breath and hold it while your heart pounds in your ears.

Thud. Thud. Thud. Ingrid hesitates at the entrance to the cave. Air rasps between her fangs, and you can picture her scanning the storm for any movement. Finally, thud, thud-thud-thud. And the heavy footfalls fade away, going deeper into the cave.

Your breath whistles out of your lungs, and dizziness clouds your vision as fresh air fills your chest. One danger avoided.

Now on to conquering the storm. The thought comes out with a lot of bravado, but as soon as you try to move, you realize just how fragile your courage is. Pain lances through you, but you try to stay positive by telling yourself that pain means blood flow.

You stomp your feet a bit to get more sensation and start looking around, trying to distinguish objects in the howling storm of white and gray.

The thought of a fire brings a warm glow to your mind, the image of rosy red flames and soft warmth while the blizzard attacks the world outside. But first you have to find such a shelter.

You head for the first hulking shape you can see only to find a spruce tree with no space beneath it in which to take refuge. Disappointment strikes hard, but you pull your cloak tighter and remind yourself you can handle this.

You move on to the next hulking shape that's barely visible through the storm. Trying to keep the icy snow away from your face, you pull your hood farther forward.

The shape's a rock, not a tree. You keep moving.

Hours later, or maybe it's only been minutes, it's hard to tell, you still haven't found a suitable tree. Your hands and feet have long since gone numb. Your nose is beyond feeling. You've tried scrunching it up repeatedly and covering it with your hand or part of your hood, but it's no use, you just can't feel it now.

You know from your woods instructor that your situation's not good. The body doesn't do well once blood stops warming its extremities.

You halt, exhausted, but then you catch the faint, homey smell of wood smoke. Sniffing deep, your heart jumps. Sure enough, it's the savory scent of a hearth fire.

A scan of the area reveals a subtle glow through the tumble of flakes and vague towers of tree trunks. As you approach, you see it's light shining through a glassed window. A warning sounds in your mind. Not many can afford glass and even fewer live in the woods because of the dangers, but you're just too cold to care.

At the door now, you hammer away until it's flung open by a woman. A wave of blessed heat washes over you from the inside, but you can't make out the woman's features because she's backlit by the room beyond.

She beckons you inside with an outstretched hand. That hand catches you moments later when you stumble on the entry rug. Unable to process what to do next, you simply stand, dripping wet from the snow

 melting on your shoulders. You shudder.

"You look positively frosty," the woman says, helping you shrug out of your cloak before guiding you to a chair by the fire. "Not too close now or you'll damage your skin. Can't feel the heat, you know."

The woman, now fully lit by the fire, is a handsome figure with flowing black hair, strong features and a deep, soothing voice. She's right, you can feel the fire, but your hands, feet, and especially your nose don't seem to be registering the warmth.

"Name's Gladys," she introduces as she brings a tub of water for your feet and another for your hands.

Gladys…Gladys…You twitch with realization. Gladys! The Woods Woman. Many call her a witch, but no one's ever proved it and she hasn't been in town in years, so she's more fable than reality.

Gladys grins and you realize your face must show your thoughts.

"Yes, that Gladys," she confirms. She kneels in front of you to inspect your nose and, from her dark eyes and the crease between her brows, you guess the prognosis isn't good.

"The tip of your nose won't return to normal," she states. "You've two options. One, go with the common Doc's remedy and remove the dead flesh. It's painful but doable. The second option's to take a tincture I can make. There's half a chance it'll turn you into a turtle, but there's also half a chance it'll revive the skin. Your call."

Gladys sits back on her heels and waits. There's no guile in her eyes despite the rough news but her options aren't perfect either way.

Have her remove the frostbite, go to page 29
If you chance the tincture, go to page 35

The old man cannot be sane. He's living with a troll and doesn't even notice the drool pooling on his shoulder. Plus, apples are common in the region, so you doubt the sweet fruit is a good bargaining chip.

You bolt for the entrance of the cave. Heavy footfalls vibrate the ground, making small stones bounce like tiny bugs on the tunnel floor. Fear forces a glance over your shoulder. Drooling fangs dominate the sight. Those fangs are made more hideous by the foul stench of breath that seeps between them to assault your nose.

Your own breath comes in heavy, chest-aching gasps as you stretch your legs for speed and fly out into the howling wind. Blinding snow pelts your face with icicles, throwing your senses into disarray.

Instead of running in a straight line, you duck to the side and twirl your cloak over you as you crouch against the side of the cave entrance. With the heavy snow, you're instantly covered in white. The weight of it pulls the cloak snug against your body.

Ingrid's heavy puffing breath alerts you to her searching. You can just imagine the foul stench seething between her teeth. She paces from left to right in an arc around the cave's mouth and her steps crunch deep into the snow. She passes beside your head, and there's a pull on the edge of your cloak as her toe presses it deeper into the snow.

You hold your breath, stilling the rasp of air in and out of your throat.

Ingrid steps again and the pull on your cloak disappears. She keeps walking, moving out farther in an ever-larger arc.

You release your breath with a slight whine that's covered by the howling wind.

It seems forever that she's looking, and all the while you shake with fear and cold. Finally she seems far enough from the cave that you might be able to slip away unnoticed. But trolls are clever and have exceptional hearing. She could just be waiting to see if you move so she can locate you.

If you stay put until the morning, you

might be able to follow your woods instructor's advice. Mister Shaffer taught you about such situations, but it's still a risk. You could get frostbite or freeze to death.

Mister Shaffer also taught you fire craft. If you wait longer and sneak to the nearest tree, you might be able to get a fire going. Snow trolls tend to avoid fire. They're not scared of the flames, but their coats catch quickly if the fire's used against them.

Slip away, go to page 41
Stay put, go to page 45
Tree and Fire, go to page 10

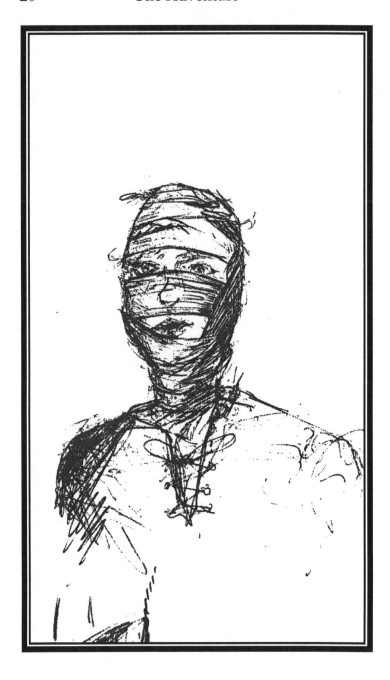

This adventure has been anything but what you imagined. You expected difficulty due to the season. Plus Moonrise Mountain isn't an easy climb, but you didn't think you'd lose parts of your skin.

Those areas ache now with a deep sensation that brings tears to your eyes.

"Home would probably be the best option," you admit, swallowing down your disappointment.

Gladys gives you an encouraging smile and nods. "All right."

***

In your mind you pictured walking home with bandages on your face and limbs. You pictured healing in your own cabin, away from the sight of the town.

In reality, Gladys keeps you in bed for several more days until your feet and hands can be uncovered and used without help. As it turns out, your hands are not nearly as bad as you expected. Your nose, Gladys warns, will be much worse, but she removes the bandage and says it'll heal on its own.

On the fifth day she leads you from her cabin to a trail she assures you will take you back to town. She hands you the bag of apples, saying, "Perhaps another time you can feed the horses."

"Thank you." You wave and start heading down the snow-covered trail.

It's not long, however, that you get a strange sense of déjà vu. Heavy clouds roll in and cover the sun. Light snow drifts to the ground, but with it comes a darker feeling to the woods.

You press forward, eager now for home. Not long later, you look back and your stomach sinks. You can see your footprints but can't tell if they're still on the trail Gladys led you to.

Going back fills you with even more dread, however. This whole adventure's been disastrous. You press on in the general direction of town and keep your head down against the snow.

You watch your feet moving forward, one step at a time, and you see immediately when your leg goes through the snow and keeps going.

You fall, tumbling head over heels into a cave that's so dark you can't see the stones that jab into you on your way down. Finally you stop and simply lie still to catch your equilibrium.

There's a shuffling sound. Your heart tries to jump out of your throat. You scramble to your feet, not wanting to face a new danger from flat on your back.

Light flares to life about ten paces ahead.

A grizzled old hand holds up a torch. With deep apprehension, you follow the hand down a bony arm. Your scrutiny stops at a scraggly beard surrounding a gap-toothed grin.

The old man coughs a laugh.

"Look, Ingrid, you were right," he says. "A snack's stumbled into your cave."

"A snack?" Your brain stumbles over that word.

There's more shuffling, and deep shadows loom behind the old man until they resolve into the heavy white-draped shoulders of a snow troll. She's a brute of a beast with a short snout and great fangs drooling saliva down her chin. Her big, intelligent eyes tighten into what might be a smile.

Those eyes look you up and down like you'd be finger licking-good, and you can't get your eyes to look away as a fresh glob of saliva drips down her fangs. She grunts and steps up to stand directly behind the old man. He doesn't seem to notice the drool that drips onto his shoulder. You shrink against the wall and the bag of apples bumps your leg.

Go to page 25 to continue.

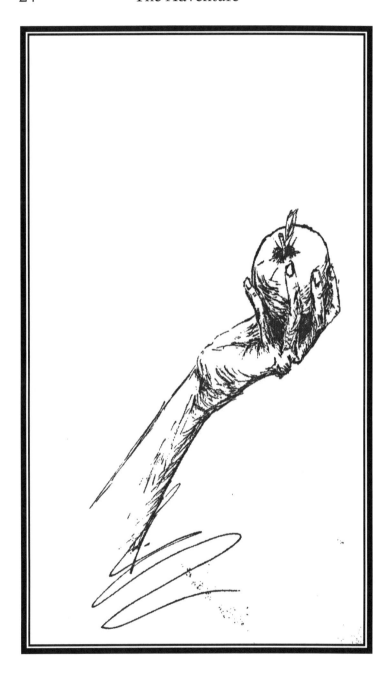

You highly doubt you can outrun a troll and the old man looks famished. You paste a grin across your lips and step farther into the light of the torch.

The old man straightens and his sparsely haired brows shoot into his hairline.

"Evening, Sir," you say in a shaky voice, "may I offer you a treat for your dinner?"

You wince at your choice of words, hoping he doesn't assume the apples are a treat to sweeten your own flavor.

You reach into the sack and pull out a shiny golden fruit. Holding it out, you wait as the apple trembles on your palm.

The old man sniffs. He steps forward and Ingrid lumbers forward at his shoulder. She leans over him to get a better look and her belly pushes him a few stumbling steps closer. He doesn't seem to mind or even notice.

The smell of the troll's breath and the old man's rank sweat assails you. Bile rises in your throat and you swallow. *Hold still.* You manage it, just barely.

Bony fingers lift the apple from your palm and cradle it gently. The old man turns the fruit right and left as he sniffs at it again, and then, with a flick of his wrist, he sends the apple sailing over his shoulder and into Ingrid's waiting maw.

Her jaws snap closed with a loud click of teeth. Crunch, crunch, crunch, and swallow. The troll's lips pull back to show all her brown teeth, and a fresh glob of saliva drips off her lower lip onto the old man's shoulder. Drops splatter your shoulders and hair.

"Ingrid approves," the old man announces. "As long as you have apples, she'll refrain from eating you." He laughs, a full body kind of laugh that shakes his frail frame like brittle leaves in a strong wind. "Here's your choice, clever one. Leave the apples and cloak and you may go unharmed. Or you may stay the night and feed Ingrid your apples.

"However, if you run out before sunlight, Ingrid will feast on you. What's your poison?"

You weigh the bag of apples and the time of day. With the storm, you're not completely sure how long you stumbled around before you fell into the cave. There might be enough apples to last until the storm abates, just barely, if your calculations are correct. If you leave now, on the other hand, without cloak or apples, you might be able to survive by following your woods instructor's advice but you might also freeze.

If you give up your cloak and apples, go to page 49

If you spend the night, go to page 55

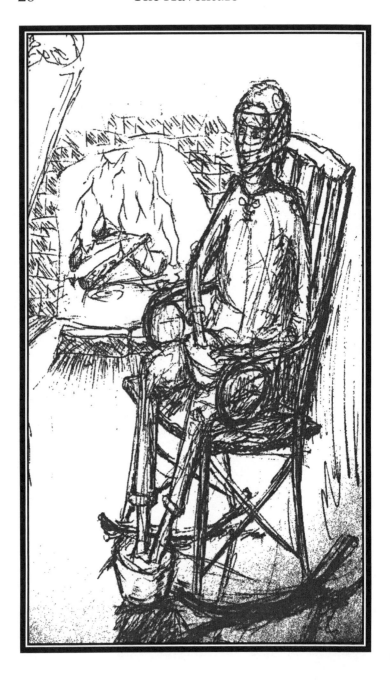

Would turning into a turtle be painful? You've no idea, but the idea of being a turtle for the rest of your life does not sound appealing. Removing the dead skin will also be painful, but safe. You cringe and tell Gladys to remove the dead skin.

Gladys accepts your choice without comment. She fills a bowl from the pot over the fire and kneels beside you on the hearthrug. In the bowl is stew and, from the smell, it's beef with vegetables.

Your mouth waters and your stomach rumbles loud enough to be heard.

Gladys chuckles. "Sorry about this but you shouldn't use your hands yet." She spoons a bite into your mouth.

The flavor of spicy beef fills your senses. It's a delicious medley that you savor with a groan. It slides down your throat and fills your belly, warming your insides with slow, delightful heat. It's then you realize just how hungry you are. Before, you knew you were cold and that silenced all other yearnings in your body. Now, your stomach claws at your insides.

You tell your fingers to move, to handle the spoon Gladys holds, but she's right about your hands. They simply sit in the water, ignoring your desire to feed yourself without aid. You can't even tell the temperature of the water.

You become aware, however, as you focus on your appendages, that although they refuse command, they are starting to tingle brutally. It reminds you of the wasp stings you've experienced from the vicious insects that appear in swarms in the summer.

You focus on the next spoonful of stew instead of the burning in your hands. The savory broth steams and fills your senses again.

"I wanted to feed the horses," you mumble around the stew. A tilt of your head toward the discarded sack of apples by the door indicates what you're talking about. There's a puddle around the sack from the snowmelt.

"Beautiful creatures," Gladys agrees.

"I've heard stories," you explain, "about feeding them and getting to ride…"

She feeds you more stew and you chew and swallow so you can continue explaining. You *have* to explain. She moves to give you another bite and, as you watch her hand holding the spoon move toward your face, you blink. The bowl and spoon have lost their clear edges. They waver like you're seeing them through a haze of steam. You blink again, but it doesn't clear your vision. If anything, the room's fuzzier.

Gladys continues to feed you. Chew, chew, swallow—

***

You wake in the same room with sunlight streaming through the glassed window. Little dust motes dance in the fingers of light. You lie on the only bed, swathed in warm blankets that smell softly of wood smoke.

Your nose itches. Sneaking a hand out, you encounter cloth instead of skin. You scrunch your nose and feel the pull of the bandage on your face.

"Ack!" You reach to remove the bandage.

"I wouldn't."

You freeze, and Gladys steps into your line of sight. Your memory of her is pretty accurate. She's a handsome woman with her long dark hair flowing freely about her shoulders.

"It will take a while to heal and exposing it won't help," she explains. "Now, I'm sorry to say this but the townspeople will not look kindly on you anymore. *"You've had dealings with the dangerous Woods Witch, you're tainted!"* She

imitates Mayor Flinn well. "I can take you to see the horses but they won't come near during this phase of the moon. You'll get to see them from afar, and then I'll return you home or..." at this she smiles and you can't help returning the expression around your awkward bandages, "you can become my apprentice, and I'll take you to see the horses when the moon's right. I can promise you many exciting discoveries but no friendship from the town."

"Or," she hesitates as though she's not even sure she should offer a third choice.

"Or?" you ask.

"You can simply go home. Your injuries will make the journey up the mountain difficult."

If you see the horses now, go to page 61

If you become Gladys's apprentice, go to page 65

If you decide to go home, go to page 21

Your fingers and toes tingle brutally as they warm in the water. It reminds you of the wasp stings you've encountered during the summer. Hundreds of wasp stings. Splinters of pain shoot into your limbs, and you don't even want to consider the pain from losing part of your nose.

"I'll try the tincture," you say.

"All right." Gladys stands. "But if you change into something unexpected, don't say I didn't warn you."

She moves around the cabin, gathering a jar from here and a mortar and pestle from another shelf. The contents of the jar join a powdery substance in the mortar, and she grinds the ingredients together, all the while humming tunelessly under her breath.

She comes back with a pasty substance and a loaf of bread. The substance smells of berries but looks similar to mashed avocado. She slathers the paste on a piece of bread she tears from the loaf and feeds it to you since your hands are still in the water. You're thankful to her because you're not sure you could move your hands if you tried.

Sweetness reminiscent of cherry pie fills your mouth, followed by a bitter twang aftertaste. Not too bad, you think, but you might just be trying to reassure yourself now that you've ingested the stuff. Gladys continues to feed you until the cherry-bitter paste is completely gone.

"Now, we wait and see," Gladys says. "Get some sleep."

She lays a blanket over you and, between it and the fire, you're toasty in no time. The pain in your extremities is now a dull ache. You're not sure if it's because of the paste or just the natural course of your body warming, but you don't fight it as your eyelids droop and sleep claims you.

***

You wake to find the room does not have the same perspective as when you went to sleep. You feel like you're viewing it from a prone position instead of from the chair. However, looking down, you see the legs of the same wooden chair you fell asleep in. The bowl of water sits on the floor but your feet do not occupy it anymore.

Even so, your hands and feet are pleasantly warm without the splinter like tingles. Perhaps you don't need the water now. You reach for your nose but find you can't get your hand around to touch your face. The muscles in your shoulder shriek that you can't move like that.

Turning your head as far as possible, you swallow convulsively but even that's slow, lethargic.

Instead of a hand and arm, you see a stubby leg and tiny claws. Pulling your legs in close to your body, you notice a domed structure on your back that weighs you down.

Wriggling slowly side to side, you confirm, sure enough, you've a shell.

Gladys kneels in front of you, but she's still towering over where you stand on the chair.

"I do try," she insists. Her words are the flap of bee wings, fast and dizzying. You shake your head. Count of three to the left, count of three to the right. Daft, but you're slow!

Gladys suddenly gets a great big grin on her face. All you can see is teeth and chin but it's a grin.

"You wanted to see the horses?" she guesses, delighted as a little girl.

Nod. Up—one, two, three. Down—one, two, three.

"As a turtle, you might be able to *hear* the stallion! But if we take the time to see him, your chance of changing back is gone," Gladys says. "Or I can try to change you back but, like before, you might become a frog or fly or something. I can take you to the horses later too. Nod to see the horses as a turtle or scrunch up if you want to attempt human form again."

Hear the stallion? That could be interesting. You've never heard of a person *hearing* an animal before, but then again, you've never spoken to someone who spent time as a turtle. Before today, you would have said it wasn't possible.

But do you want to spend the rest of your life as a turtle? Slow and unable to scratch your nose forever? Gladys did say she'd take you to see the horses as a human too.

Even your thinking feels slow as you consider your options. Staying a turtle could be quite an adjustment.

If you nod, go to page 69
If you scrunch, go to page 73

Your toes are going numb and the tip of your nose lost sensation a while ago. As hard as you try, staying still *and* warm doesn't go hand-in-hand.

Straining your ears, you can just make out the crunch of heavy footfalls over the howl of the storm. They are a dull thud more felt than heard in the ground beneath you.

Ingrid must be some ways away and with the blowing, shrieking snow, the likelihood of her seeing or hearing you is even slimmer than normal. Although her senses are much sharper than your own, this gives you a glimmer of hope.

You peek out from under your cloak. Snow dumps into your face, and you barely keep an 'ugh' from escaping you. Blinking away the flakes stuck to your lashes, you make out the dark, hulking form of the troll. She is indeed a ways off, stalking the dark like she can track you even in the weather's fury, but she's too far away to actually be on your trail.

This gives the glimmer of hope added fuel.

Shaking a little, you test your limbs to make sure all's well. Although your feet are cold, they don't seem to have fallen asleep.

You stand and take a wobbly step, and then another, and then you run. Although your legs aren't asleep, they don't work quite as you hoped. You should feel the cold and the thud of your steps, but all you get is a dull ache in your flesh. Snow shifts and rocks turn under your feet. You stumble as the lack of sensation makes it hard to judge your stride or to compensate for the uncertain footing.

Two steps later and there's an ear-splitting roar. Compared to the howl of the storm, it's a piercing shriek instead of a mind-numbing wail. Ingrid's seen you. Ugly troll has better senses than you bargained for! Even with the wind biting and whistling past your ears, her heavy strides thud, clear and gaining, behind you.

Attempting to run faster only makes you stumble again. Your feet fumble against each other, and you grasp a tree to steady yourself. Your hands shake where they hold the rough trunk of the pine.

Glancing back, you shriek and pitch the apples at the troll. She sweeps the flying bag aside and keeps coming.

With a push against the tree, you strain to reach the edge of the forest. Maybe you can make it.

A sharp-clawed paw catches your shoulder and spins you around. You try to duck away, but she's got your cloak in her grasp and the garment holds you fast.

Unfortunately, the rest of your story is too horrible to tell. May you rest in peace.

The End

The cold seeps into your limbs, an insidious, creeping foe that threatens to numb you to the world permanently. You push the fear gnawing in your gut down and remind yourself Mister Shaffer, your woods instructor, taught you about such situations in his lessons on survival.

You might be able to slip away but you doubt it. Trolls have uncannily sharp senses and, even with the storm, she's likely to pick up the sound of your running feet. And if Ingrid notices you, there's no way you'll outrun her in the deep snow. It's a miracle enough that you went unnoticed up to this point.

You wiggle your toes, flex your calves, and then move to your thighs. In this fashion, you move through your whole body and start again. Wiggle toes, flex calves—constant, subtle motion. Just enough for blood flow. It's painful in your numb limbs, but the sharp pricks of sensation encourage you that you haven't lost blood flow to those areas.

Once you get a sort of rhythm to it, you move on to slowly, ever so slowly, burrowing deeper into the snow.

There's a sniffling sound and you freeze. A heavy thump next to your head makes you jump. Ingrid's foot catches the edge of your cloak again, and it pulls tight across your shoulders.

This creates a pulling sensation around your neck, and you struggle for air. Panic almost makes you pull away.

Don't move, don't move!

The scrape of claws against stone and another thump sends the fear gnawing at your gut into your throat, tightening your already restricted airflow. Ingrid's next step, though, releases the edge of your cloak and your chest expands in a deep, relief-giving breath.

You listen with strained ears until Ingrid's thudding steps indicate she's entered the cave again. The thump-thump sound stops just inside, and you imagine her watching from the cover of the cave's mouth.

You start your routine of wiggle, flex, flex, and burrow until you're well into the snow again.

In order not to suffocate, you peek out from under your cloak. Snow plasters itself across your skin where it melts from the warmth on your face. You dab the skin dry before hollowing out a slanted hole that butts up against the rock of the cave. It's not big but it is enough to let blessed air into your cocoon. Mister Shaffer would be proud.

You return to wiggling toes, flexing muscles, and waiting for daylight to rescue you from Ingrid's wrath. Sharp tingles in your limbs reassure you blood still flows in your extremities. It's a constant sensation of pain that, for once in your life, you fully welcome.

Hours later as the snow lets up, sharp rays of sunshine begin to peek through your ventilation hole. Those beautiful fingers of light bring tears to your eyes.

You're stiff, sore and half frozen but still alive and, with the sun, you safely head back to the cabin to warm up and check yourself for frostbite. Perhaps another day you'll reach the top of Moonrise Mountain.

The End

Although it's dark outside, you suspect it's due to the storm and not the time of day. Sunshine would hold Ingrid at bay, but it could be days before you see any of the beautiful light through the vicious storm. Plus, there are definitely not enough apples for more than a few hours.

You lower the bag to the floor while keeping your eyes on the oddly matched pair. Ingrid's eyes follow the bag and stay on it as you shrug out of your cloak and set it on the floor as well. Immediately the lack of warmth and the comforting weight on your shoulders is missed.

With a slight bow, you bid the old man and troll a good day. The old man's cackle follows you out of the cave until you reenter the storm, and the howl of the wind overpowers his voice.

At least the troll didn't follow. The knot in your stomach loosens just a little as the looming creature stays behind.

One danger down, your mind moves on to the next problem. The bite of the wind and snow stings your skin with icy blasts. It's a daunting experience to stare into a blustering storm so thick you can't see ten feet in front of your face, but you square your shoulders and move forward.

Don't give in, don't give up. This mantra sticks in your mind, repeating over and over. Your woods instructor, Mister Shaffer, taught you how to survive such situations and you're no quitter.

With Mister Shaffer's advice guiding you, you look for a large pine tree. Without your cloak, you need to find somewhere to stay warm fast. You need a sheltered spot to start a fire. At least you hope you can get a fire going.

Don't give in, don't give up. Cold eats at your fingers and nose.

The blowing white shifts every shape into unidentifiable objects until you get close. The first hulking shape turns out to be a rock instead of the tree you need. The second turns out to be several young trees covered in snow but lacking any sheltered space beneath. Finally, on your third try, you find a large pine with low-hanging branches.

You crawl on your belly under the branches and find a more sheltered area underneath in which you can actually sit up. It's exactly perfect.

Above your head, hanging off the tree limbs, is a priceless treasure in your situation.

Old man's beard. The fibrous moss works as a great fire starter. Gathering as much of it as you can, you collect it into a pile.

Sadly, you didn't bring a flint. When you left the cabin that morning, it didn't even occur to you that you might need a way to light a fire.

Thankfully, in the shelter of the pine, you also find some deadwood. You select a flatter piece and notch out a small divot with a rock. Next, you take the straightest stick you can find, fit the end into the divot and begin to twirl the stick between your palms.

You've done this once before and know well the time and strength it requires. You push the daunting thought from your mind and keep going. You've done this before, it can be done.

Don't give in, don't give up. The thought holds a glimmer of hope.

Tediously, you keep the stick moving, pressing down as you go. The mere effort warms you enough that sweat trickles down your sides. Finally blessed smoke dances into the air around your stick.

Relief escapes your throat in the form of a tiny laugh. With hands blistered and arms sore, you blow gently at the smoke until it springs to life in your tinder of moss and small twigs. Fire!

By the time the sun returns, you've a small fire going and a chunk of dry dirt to sit on. You've spent the night keeping the fire alive while the boughs of the tree kept your heat in and the snow off.

You're not horribly comfortable, but you're alive and can attempt Moonrise Mountain another day. Mister Shaffer would be proud!

The End

Time, no matter what decision you make, is working against you. There aren't a lot of apples. It would be a gamble to hope they'd last long enough for the sun to rescue you.

On the other hand, the entire world outside the cave lies in snow and howls with cold. Giving up your cloak would be inviting a death sentence—unless you could find a sheltered spot quickly in which to light a fire. Although you've had survival training, you doubt you'd survive long enough to find such a shelter.

You pull your cloak tighter, square your shoulders, and give the old man a look of defiance as you approach.

He laughs, his whole body shaking in clear delight, and leads the way farther into the cave where he has a small fire crackling.

You and Ingrid follow. She walks next to you, and with every step her foul breath ruffles the hair on the top of your head. This produces the image of drool hanging from her fat lips.

Sure enough, a cold drop lands in your hair. Cringing, you tighten your hold on the apples. The drool slides down through your hair and onto your neck. You keep from wiping it away by reminding yourself you don't want to offend the troll and have her eat you, apples and all.

Ingrid shuffles around to the old man's side of the fire and lowers her massive bulk to a sprawled sitting position. She's just far enough away from the fire to keep it from igniting her heavy fur. You settle down as well, across from the old man and troll, and securely set the bag of apples in your lap. Pulling one out, you proceed to polish it on your shirt.

"What's your name?" you ask the old man.

He cackles. "Can't remember. Ingrid can't say a name."

He continues, rambling about Ingrid being the best companion in the world. While he's talking, you slowly, non-threateningly, reach for the knife you noticed a moment before sitting on the stones next to the fire. It's nothing sharp that you could use against the troll, but it gives you an idea. You slice the apple into quarters, then eighths, not bothering to slice out the core. Ingrid doesn't seem to mind the core anyway.

Her great eyes watch and she snorts with glee when you toss her a piece. She throws her whole body into catching the apple on her tongue. This sends drool everywhere, but considering it prolongs the process, you'll take the drool.

"How'd you end up here?" you ask to keep the old man talking.

"Fate!" he exclaims. Then he tells you a stilted, incomprehensible tale about Ingrid, hated gofers, and a slouched hat he lost. You can't make the right of it no matter how you try, but you continue to ask questions like it's the most fascinating tale you've ever encountered.

The time passes with you scrounging for questions and the old man giving you off-the-wall, unintelligible answers. His eyes sparkle with glee at every chance to tell you more about his companion.

All the while, you cut apples and toss the pieces to Ingrid. Her heavy crunch as she bites each one punctuates the old man's flailing arms as he tells you stories.

"See, there we stood…" Crunch. "…minding the trees…" The old man keeps rambling as you toss another slice. Crunch.

It's about the time you reach the last apple that you see the flaw in this situation. You're deep in the cave and can't see the sun, even if it is shining. A deep knot of fear threatens to choke you.

The old man and troll haven't realized yet you're on your last apple because of the way the bag's settled in your lap.

Well into his newest rambling, the old man's on his back with his arms waving about. Ingrid's eyeing the last two pieces of apple in your hand. You keep your eyes on the old man and suddenly toss both chunks high into the air in two different directions. Ingrid shrieks in consternation, a snorting, snot-flying cry as she can't catch both pieces on her tongue, but you're already on your feet running.

There's a growl of anger and Ingrid's after you. You hear a stutter step as she avoids the fire, but then her heavy steps shake the floor under your feet when she lengthens her strides to make up the difference.

An involuntary cry of hope escapes your throat as you round the corner and see faint light at the mouth of the cave. Its soft glow tells you the day's more than half over, but there's still daylight to brighten the sky.

Just then you trip, coming down hard on your palms, but it saves your life as Ingrid's claws miss and screech against the cave wall above your head.

Scrambling to your feet again, you strain your legs and fly out into the blessed sunlight.

Ingrid screams a deafening howl of fury that makes all sound disappear for a good couple seconds, but you don't stop until you're well away from the mouth of the cave. When you look back, Ingrid's still screaming her frustration, but she's well tucked into the cave, out of the light of day.

Relief washes over you, even more

dizzying than the lack of sound just moments before. With light steps, you head home, exhausted and out of apples, but alive.

The End

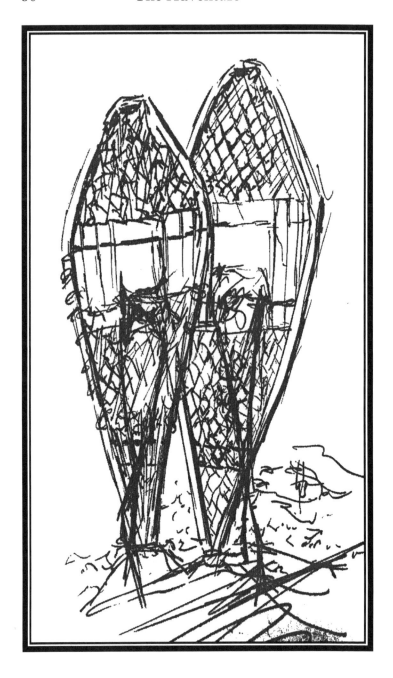

The cold of the storm sapped your desire for adventure, but the stubborn part of you refuses to go home before at least seeing the horses you came to find.

"I'd like to go see the horses now," you respond to Gladys's question. Her eyes look sad but she doesn't argue.

After a few days of recovery, Gladys outfits you with a pair of snowshoes and leads you up Moonrise Mountain along a winding path buried beneath a layer of glistening white.

Breath puffs in and out of your lungs as the heavy snow pulls at your legs. For having frostbite a few days before, you're experiencing a lot of painful sensation through your legs and in your chest from the hike. It brings an odd mix of pleasure and dismay. You can still feel everything, but you're dissatisfied in the condition of your body. By the time you reach the meadow near the summit, it's well past noon, and you're plastered with sweat, breathing like a bellows.

But all of this is forgotten as you see the herd.

Closest to you stands a gray stallion. His broad shoulders and arched neck stand well above those of the tame herds you've seen in town.

Behind him lie several mares, and farther

out prance two yearling colts.

"The full herd is a lot bigger, but they only gather at the full moon," Gladys informs you.

You don't mind. The few horses you see project such spirit, such beauty, that a part of your adventurous spirit returns. All you want to do is sit and watch, to take in their majesty as a boon to your sore soul.

After a time, you open the bag of apples you insisted on bringing that morning and regretted on your hike up for their weight. Now you're glad you carried them.

You place two of the golden apples onto of the snow and step back to wait.

One colt charges forward to investigate, but a warning snort from the stallion stops him short in a shower of hooves and fresh snow.

They graze and play a while longer until the stallion turns toward you and paws the air.

Gladys touches your shoulder. "He's had enough. It's time to go."

You reluctantly turn away and follow her from the meadow. It's well after dark by the time you reach the cabin.

***

You walk the main street in town, listening to the thud of your shoes on the boardwalk. You'd look up, but after a few months at home, you've found the townspeople just give you dark looks. You've had dealings with the *Woods Witch*.

Someone bumps your shoulder.

"Sorry," you say out of reflex but don't look up.

"Hi," a voice says, "I'm Stanley."

You look up, shocked, to find a boy holding out his hand in greeting. "What happened to your nose?"

You hesitate, but he's not giving you a dark look—he's just curious. You explain and his eyes light up with a spark of adventurous glee that you recognize. He goes with you one day to find Gladys but you don't succeed. The cabin isn't where you remember it.

You and Stanley become close friends, and to this day you talk about seeing the wild herd again. You like to think the stallion ate the apples after you left. It's a nice thought, but someday you'd like him to eat from your hand. Someday...

The End

Gladys is right. You won't be accepted at home any more. Even if your interaction with the *Woods Witch* didn't taint you in the eyes of the townsfolk, the scarring on the end of your nose would surely turn you into an outcast.

Although Gladys is considered a witch by the town, no one argues her intelligence and knowledge. Those traits are some of the very reasons people fear her. She could have a lot to teach you, plus you'll get to see the wild horses up close. It's a win-win choice considering your options.

"I'll be your apprentice," you say.

Gladys' face transforms into a splitting grin.

She gives you a few days to recover and starts to teach you about the dried plants she has hanging around the cabin. About Queen Anne's Lace and Cattails, about Lamb's Quarters and Thyme...

When the night turns dark with the full moon barely peaking over the edge of the horizon, Gladys wakes you and hands you a pair of snowshoes and a sack of apples. She nearly glows with excitement.

You follow her through the night up a winding trail still covered by heavy snow. Soft clouds cover the face of the moon, keeping its light from gilding the night in silver. Above, the stars glitter in the sky like millions of gems on a black velvet canvas.

By the time you reach the meadow near the top of Moonrise Mountain, you're no longer watching the sky but are bent over, drenched in sweat and puffing for breath.

But you enter the meadow and halt. The clouds have now drifted away and the light of the moon reveals the meadow. Before you, not five feet away, stands a gray stallion. His shoulders top your head and his neck arches at your appearance. You scramble for an apple and hold one in your trembling palm.

He approaches and his nostrils snuffle your offering. Warm breath accompanies the soft tickle of his lips as he investigates what you hold on the palm of your hand. With a loud crunch, he takes the apple. You can almost hear him hum in satisfaction.

"Give him another," Gladys whispers.

You spend the night feeding the stallion and a few mares he'll let come close enough. By the time the sun peaks over the edge of the horizon, you're out of apples and are happy with life.

***

You spend the rest of your life learning from Gladys and visiting the wild herd. It's several years later that the stallion bends a knee and allows you to climb onto his back.

The ride's wild with wind snipping at your ears and your hands clutching at his mane just to stay on. You never direct him, you just ride, but when you get news randomly from town, they say there's a new horseman, riding the wild herd like a hero of old.

The End

Hearing the stallion sounds intriguing. You're not sure exactly what Gladys means, but it's worth checking out. You nod sluggishly. Up, one-two-three, down, one-two-three.

Gladys claps, throws together a small pack with food and extra clothing, and then sets you atop the pack's top flap behind her right shoulder.

"Stay very still," she advises as she heads out of the cabin.

The day's coated in sunshine and fresh white snow that sparkles with ice crystals. It'd be a captivating sight except for the motion sickness that threatens in your throat.

Your stomach rolls with every step Gladys takes. You breathe deep until, after the first half hour or so, everything finally settles enough for you to enjoy the ride.

Unlike before, you don't feel the cold much. The heat from Gladys' shoulder and the sun striking your shell are more than enough to warm you.

Gladys' strides are long and powerful, and before long she's carried you to a meadow near the summit of Moonrise Mountain. Even the snowshoes on her feet don't slow her much. You marvel that her breathing isn't labored. You're sure, if you'd just made the same climb, you'd be puffing like a bellows.

Entering the meadow, you hear a deep snort and a *heads up*!

Before you stands a gray stallion whose shoulders top Gladys's head. His great dark eyes scan Gladys until they come to rest on you. There's a lot of intelligence behind those long-lashed eyes.

You stretch out your neck and arch it until your nose touches Gladys' shoulder. It just seems like the right thing to do.

You're not turtle born, says the deep voice.

How do you respond? You can't talk, not like you used to anyway. You settle for a three-count shake of your head.

A deep, chest-vibrating laugh answers you. *So be it,* says the stallion, *would you like a spin?*

Would you ever! But riding on Gladys was hard enough. Can turtles puke? Ah, who cares! You nod.

The stallion bows a knee and Gladys chuckles her surprise.

"Making friends fast, eh? It's not even the right phase of the moon for the stallion to come close." She's clearly delighted as she sets you on the stallion's broad shoulders. You bite a mouthful of mane as he rises.

We'll walk first.

You heartily agree, seeing as how his walk's faster than you can now run. You soon find riding Heath, the stallion, your favorite thing to do.

You and Heath become fast friends as Gladys surmised.

Gladys carries you to the meadow a few times a week and leaves you to discuss the world's issues with your best friend. Issues such as where do falling stars land and how does the melted snow return to the sky for the next winter. You couldn't ask for a happier life and, after a while, you don't care that you're a turtle. In fact, what do human's know? They move too fast anyway.

The End

You can't imagine handling life as a turtle. The very idea of always moving slowly fills you with deep choking dread. You scrunch up tight into your shell.

Gladys sighs. "I'll try."

She stands and again putters around while humming tunelessly. This time it seems incredibly fast, like she's prancing along, and you close your eyes tight to keep the movement from sickening your stomach. Can turtles throw up? You don't know.

The smell of fresh fish finds your nose and, although it's uncooked, your stomach rumbles with hunger.

Gladys sets a small plate before you with the fish and an unknown sort of seasoning. You've very little knowledge of fish but you're pretty sure eating it raw isn't a good idea.

You pull your head back into your shell.

"Go ahead," Gladys encourages, "eat. It won't hurt you." She smiles and pushes the plate closer.

Maybe as a turtle raw fish isn't so bad. You give it a sniff, but it smells as bad to you as a turtle as it does when you're human. You hold your breath while you take your first bite.

You nibble away a tiny bit at a time until your stomach doesn't hurt with hunger. It takes a while because your tongue and mouth feel unwieldy, and bits of fish dribble down your chin.

There's a pop. You gasp as wings sprout where before you had a shell. Your neck expands and great long teeth press into your lips. You're powerful and mighty with beautiful wings. Colors shimmer and glow around you in vibrant clarity.

The raven color of Gladys' hair shines as she moves, and the sun sparkles through the windows like liquid gold.

"Ooh, a young dragon!" Gladys exclaims, but she's not afraid, just excited.

Pop! Your wings disappear, your teeth become blocky, and the world dulls.

You look down and groan in half relief and half disappointment. You're human again, and the raw fish truly smells rancid. You swallow hard, just barely keeping your stomach in place.

Gladys clears out the fish, all the while surmising the combination that created a dragon. She feeds you a lunch of bread, cheese, and hardboiled eggs and directs you how to get home.

"Come back at the full moon and I'll get you to Moonrise Mountain."

You readily agree after this adventure.

At the full moon you return, and Gladys takes you to see the wild horses. They're great beasts with high shoulders, coats ranging in all possible colors (you wonder how they'd look to a dragon) and wild spurts of energy that send them flying over the ground.

You return at each full moon and eventually get a few to eat from your hand, but they never bend a knee for you to ride.

"I've only seen them let someone ride once," Gladys says. "It took the man several years before that happened, too. I wouldn't worry about it."

You shrug. In reality, you're more bothered with how dull your world is now. You can't get the vibrant world as seen through a dragon's eyes out of your head.

If you ever get past the smell of raw fish, you plan to ask Gladys to change you back. You'd dearly love to be a dragon again.

The End

The Adventure
of the
Temple of Night and Wind
Jennifer M Zeiger

Illustrated by
Justin Allen

"This is a bad idea," William hisses. It's a soft sound, but since he's right at your ear, you feel his breath as he speaks.

"Shhh," you say. "This is my best course of action."

Even as you say the words, shivers tighten the muscles in your back until you struggle to remain still. Only years of hunting actually keep you from giving in to your body's reaction.

"There's got to be a better way," William insists.

"I'm listening if you've figured it out," you say, "but I can't return to the village tonight without food again, not when everyone's starving."

William grumbles but doesn't actually say anything. He knows you're right.

"I'm not going in with you," he finally says.

"I know," you say, but you're not really listening. Instead, you're staring at the cave, reminding yourself that this *is* your best course of action.

Around you lies a boulder field. Beyond that, the forest grows thick, obscuring anything more than five feet in any direction.

The cave sits tucked deep within the mass of rocks that sprout like moles from the forest floor. It's low to the ground and almost hidden from sight, but the longer you stare at it, the more you can see. The outline of it gaps with jagged edges similar to a feline's sharp-toothed smile. It's the Howling Maw.

"It eats people," William reminds you.

You scoff. "People just say that."

"What happened to Lawrence, then?" he asks.

You don't have an answer. Lawrence entered the cave when the village first started having problems. A friend watched him enter, and he waited for him to return. He waited, and waited awhile longer. Finally, he gave up, and Lawrence hasn't been seen since. He's not the first one to disappear into the Maw either.

But there are tales about the cave. They weave enticing promises about the person who makes it back alive. They say you can find riches beyond your imagination.

You're not a treasure hunter, and usually you wouldn't even think about entering the Howling Maw, but the village is in trouble. For months now the crops have been failing, a lack of rain turning everything a sickly brown. You feel the gnawing of hunger in your belly even now. To substitute the failing crops, the village asked you and the other hunters to bring in more meat.

But deer and rabbit have proved just as

scarce as good crops. No water for the crops equals no water for the animals, and they're smart enough to head elsewhere for survival.

All day you've been out hunting, but your belt hangs empty of game. Other villages turned to buying their food from the city. Your village is poor, though, and buying food is not an option—unless you defeat the Howling Maw.

You grit your teeth. If the Maw can feed your people, you've reached the point where you'll chance the danger.

"Bad idea," William repeats, as though reading your thoughts.

You hold out your hands to emphasize your empty belt. No game hangs there, and his belt is no better than yours.

His dark eyes are sad as he shakes his head.

"Wait for me?" you ask him.

"Give you the traditional three days," he says.

"Good," you say. You check the hunting bow that hangs comfortably over your shoulder. It's just a stalling tactic. At your side hangs your knife. You're better armed than most in the village, but it's still scant reassurance as you build up the courage to enter.

With a deep breath and a last long look

at the sun above, you slap William on the shoulder before venturing down into the cave. His voice calls a last, "Three days, that's all," and the echo of it follows you as the Maw opens to surround you in darkness.

You trail a hand along the right wall while your other hand rests on the bow. The floor slopes down, and gravel crunches on stone at every step. Through the soft soles of your shoes, the stone bites with tiny nibbles. The sound of your breath echoes softly as a rasp. It mingles with the crunch of your stride to create a rough duet in a place where no sounds should intrude.

A cool wind picks up, fluttering against your face. It creates a low moan, as though the Maw is waking to your presence. As you continue on, you blink, but your eyes aren't playing tricks. A wavering light breaks the darkness up ahead.

You round a corner and come to a stop, shocked. A torch sits burning in a wall bracket. It illuminates two possible ways. A knot settles, tight and heavy, into your stomach.

To the left, the floor slants down with deep cuts. Stairs? Here? But there's no mistaking the grooves cut by a pickaxe. The wind howls up those stairs and blows your hair with its strength. On the air you think you hear whispered voices. A shiver runs your spine.

To the right stands a heavy wooden door with iron bands crossing the thick planks. In the small crack below the door, firelight flickers from the other side.

Voices in one direction and firelight in the other. You swallow. Both ways indicate you might encounter someone when you did not expect to find signs of life.

To go left down the stairs, flip to page 85
To go right through the door, flip to page 131

The firelight dancing beneath the edge of the door is a sure sign somebody's home. The voices, on the other hand, might be a trick of the wind. At least you really hope it's a trick of the wind.

You grab the torch from the wall and descend the stone stairs. They're old and worn with grit covering their surface. The rounded edges on each step make you picture your foot sliding from beneath you, and you tumbling head over heels down the dark passage.

You move slowly, making sure of each step before you weight your foot. Even with your cautious movement, your steps still crunch on the stone. With the wind, however, the sound's more a feeling through your feet than an audible noise.

The stairs come to an end, and the tunnel takes a sharp right turn. You peek around the turn but don't see much other than faint light. So you step around and find, now that the stone of the tunnel isn't in your way, a large cavern. You're standing in a sort of entryway that flares out into the larger room. The ceiling above has a big hole through which the wind howls with deafening fury.

You're suddenly very glad for that hole, because without it, your torch would be the only light in a very occupied room. As it is, only the first few creatures, the ones nearest you, have noticed your arrival. They stare at you over heavy shoulders.

Shoulders made entirely of stone. The creatures are squat and round but completely made of rock. When one turns to look, its neck crunches with a deep rumbling. Not many are standing, but the few that are only reach your shoulders in height. The rest sit in small groups muttering to each other. That explains the voices you heard on the wind. It's a faint sound even where you stand now, almost like they're all whispering at once.

Across the cavern giant pillars rise, cut into the wall. Your skin prickles and your hair stands on end. Between the pillars is an entryway with doors thrown wide open. That entry would easily fit a man ten feet tall. Not that you've ever seen a man that tall, but then again, you've never seen stone men before, so you're not about to discount anything at this point.

You look back up the stairs, considering abandoning your insane idea of coming back with riches. Dismay makes you utter a low cry. You slap a hand over your mouth to keep the sound from carrying too far.

There's a closed gate between you and the first step now. You didn't see it when you passed by, and there was no rattle when it closed. How did it close? Did you walk over a pressure plate or past a tripwire? There's no lever to open it on this side either. You can see a lever beyond, higher on the stairs, but it's well beyond your reach.

You turn back and step softly into the giant cavern. The chill wind surrounds you as  more stone heads grind around to look in a motion so slow you wonder if it pains them. The stone faces don't allow for much expression. You can't tell if they grimace or smile a greeting.

Goose flesh covers your arms at the eerie sight of stone eyes watching you. You can't tell if their eyes move separate from their heads, but from the ones closest to you, you can tell they don't have pupils. Just perfectly round stone orbs where a human's eyes sit.

Perhaps you could run through the room faster than these creatures can respond, whatever they are. You might be able to get to that far entry before they move to hinder you, but there are a lot of them. You'd be dodging them along the way.

Plus, you really have no idea how fast they can move or if they'll try to hinder you in the first place. Maybe if you move slowly, unthreatening-like, they might let you pass. They might not even notice your motion.

If you sprint for the entry, flip to page 97
If you walk for the far side, flip to page 115

You pull your knife to test putting it into the light of a prism. It deflects the prism onto the ceiling. There's a gritty pop, and a shower of dust fills the air.

You realize that, not only might it catch you on fire, it might explode as well. Nope. Not something you want to chance. You go back to the tiny side tunnel you saw earlier.

It truly is at the minimum of what you might fit through, but without your bow, you might be able to slide free. There's faint light at the far end that encourages you on.

You inhale a steadying breath and enter the tunnel. No longer are you able to crawl. Now you're pushing with your toes and pulling against the rough stone with the palms of your hands to move yourself forward.

This motion scrapes at your skin and pulls at your cloths, but there's a bare couple inches that allow you to slide along. If you escape the Maw, you're going to look like it chewed on you.

When you reach the middle and feel the stone pressing tight against your sides, you look ahead. The tunnel slants upward, and there's more light showing the closer you get to the end. You're almost there.

With a pull of your palms, you inch forward and pause. Your pocket grows hot, and you hear a rip as the book *Below the Cavern* tears free and flies back down the tunnel from which you came.

Then, before you can truly contemplate its loss, your fingers feel something familiar but strange beneath your palms instead of the stone floor. Before your eyes, a bow forms. It's smaller than the one burned up by the prisms, but the wood is the same. Relief so intense it brings tears to your eyes fills you. This is the weapon you're most skilled with.

Apparently the Maw is vicious, and generous.

You grip the bow and proceed forward until you can peek your head out of the tunnel. What you see outside makes you pause.

The room beyond is a giant cavern and it's full of people. The roof contains a big hole

through which the wind howls with deafening fury, but it also allows in light for you to see by.

There are a few occupants near you sitting on the floor. They must have noticed you peeking from the tunnel because they've glanced over their shoulders.

Shoulders entirely made of stone. The creatures are squat and round but completely made of stone. When one turns to look, its neck crunches with a deep rumbling.

To the left of your spot, you make out giant pillars cut into the wall. Your skin prickles and your hair stands on end. Between the pillars is an entryway with doors thrown wide open.

To the right of your spot is another tunnel, but you can just make out a gate closing off that option.

The stone people who originally noticed you seem to have lost interest and have gone back to their whispered conversation.

You slowly pull yourself from the tunnel and breathe deep at the relief to be free of it. That relief, however, is tinged with concern as your motion draws the attention again of those in the room. Even more give notice as a torch flares to life beside you on the wall. Stone heads grind around to look in a motion so slow you wonder if it pains them. The faces don't allow for expression. You can't tell if they grimace or smile a greeting.

Goose flesh covers your arms at the eerie sight of stone eyes watching you. You can't tell if their eyes move separate from their heads but, from the ones closest to you, you can tell they don't have pupils. Just perfectly round stone orbs where a human's eyes sit.

You pull the torch off the wall and raise it high to get a clearer look at the room.

Perhaps you could run through the room faster than these creatures can respond. You might be able to get to that tall entry before they hinder you, but there are a lot of them. You'd be dodging them along the way.

Plus, you really have no idea how fast they can move or if they'll try to hinder you in the first place. Maybe if you move slowly, unthreatening-like, they might let you pass. They might not even notice your motion.

If you sprint for the entry, flip to page 97
If you walk for the far side, flip to page 115

Your nerves are about shot at this point. Your knuckles have lost their color where they grip your bow.

Every year in the village, the people host contests in the spring between all the hunters. Races, archery, spear throwing. You win your share of them, but in sprinting, you win the majority of the time.

That speed could be useful in getting through the cavern. The creature's slow head movements are a good indication that all of their movements will probably be slow. You take off for the other side, dodging a zigzag path over boulders and around stone creatures. The pump of your legs feels good, burning the excess, nervous energy from your body.

For the first few strides nothing happens.

Then there's a heavy rumbling that shakes the ground beneath your feet. The whispers of conversation grow louder until they're shouts that bounce off the cavern walls. Excitement, urgency, desperate need. All of these emotions seem to infuse the shouting to create a cacophony of sound ringing in your ears.

A stone hand swings into your path faster than you imagined possible. Getting hit by that arm would probably knock you completely senseless. You duck but the bow over your shoulder catches, swinging you backward like a doll. The bow flies from your shoulder as you tumble but somehow you manage to retain your hold on the torch without burning yourself.

You crash into another stone figure, and those heavy arms grind shut to embrace you.

At the last second before you're pulled into that mighty stone hug, you slip down into a crouch and duck away. You raise the torch in a defensive posture.

Only to find yourself in a ring of stone people. They stand shoulder-to-shoulder with no room to squeeze between them. Dozens of stone eyes stare at you and you sway in place, your breath puffing through your lips.

A stone hand shoots outward and you flinch back, but it's only offering the bow back to you. In your tumble, you had completely lost track of it. Guess they have no reason to keep it since it can't hurt them.

You take the bow, and the one who handed it to you mouths a sound. A dusty rasp emerges like it's clearing its throat. After a moment of lip movement but no sound, the word "human" rumbles out.

"Yes," you say, "I'm human."

All of the stone heads turn side to side. With that many moving at once, the grinding rumbles the floor.

The creature repeats "human," with a hand to its chest.

"You're human?" you ask.

They all nod and pebbles bounce around on the ground. They point to the tall entryway. "Death to stone," they rumble. "Human flesh beyond."

What?

"You can't pass the entryway?" you guess.

They shake their heads.

"But I can?"

Nods.

"Human flesh returns in Merriam's Light. Bring back Light," the spokesman says. The stone circle opens to allow you through. You step between them, still unnerved by all of this, and approach the entry with the massive pillars.

A glance back proves they're all watching with eager expressions. One motions for you to go on past the entry.

You step through.

There's a flash, and the wall in front lights up with two images. One looks like a star and the other like a sword. You raise the torch higher to see more.

A voice asks, "Stargazer or Searcher?"

The stone people want you to bring back Merriam's Light in order for them to return to their human form. At least, that's what you guess they want.

You've no reason to think they're tricking you, but is Merriam's Light a star?

It occurs to you that the only real stars possible in the Howling Maw are the ones seen through the hole in the top of the cavern. Saying "Stargazer" could send you back to the cavern instead of putting you on the right path to Merriam's Light.

But what about "Searcher?" And what about the sword? Could the searcher mean you're searching for Merriam's Light?

Questions spin through your head, but the wall only waits for you to decide.

If you say Stargazer, flip to page 103
If you say Searcher, flip to page 109
If you ask for time to consider, flip to page 155

Maybe Merriam's Light is considered a star, and where there's a star, there might be the treasure you're hoping to find. Excitement builds within you at the possibility of success.

"Stargazer," you answer.

The corresponding star on the wall lights up, and you feel an odd tingling run over your skin.

"Stargazer," the voice repeats. "To stone you turn until a time when human flesh brings Merriam's Light to touch your skin. You will gaze above at the stars that could save you but not without the wizard's crystal."

The excitement turns to dread. Something just went terribly wrong—you're sure of it. The tingling on your skin intensifies, and you look at your hands as they become heavy and clumsy. Your fingers round out into digits of stone.

OH NO!

The wind kicks up into a mighty, howling tempest that buffets your chest. Your torch snuffs out, and the howling force drives you back into the cavern. You fight it but trip over your heavy stone feet.

Landing on your back, you look up into the sad eyes of several stone men. As opposed to before, you can clearly make out the expression on their faces.

"I'm Laawreeencce," the man says.

Lawrence?

It dawns on you. The tanner's son who disappeared months ago. Now you know what happened to him.

"You aall were once huumaan?" you ask.

Lawrence nods and starts pointing out people you know from the village.

"If we pass the tall arch like this," Lawrence goes on to explain, "we will turn to dust."

He explains that to return to human form, you need the crystal that rests in Wizard Merriam's hands in the temple beyond the arch. When starlight passes through the crystal to land on you, it changes you back.

A deep sense of longing fills you. As a stone person, everything is dulled. You can't feel the cool wind on your face or the sharpness of the stone beneath your feet. You try, after you see a few others do it, to chew on some of the rocks. They simply fill your mouth with dust. With a chuckle at your disgusted face, Lawrence explains you don't require food. So you gaze through the top of the cavern at the stars and wait for another human to pass through.

Your thoughts move sluggishly while you wait. Too slow, you realize later, when a human passes carefully by. Only after his soft steps have passed and he's gone from the cavern do you realize you've missed the opportunity to speak with him.

The disappointment on your face must tell Lawrence of your mood. He lowers himself to sit beside you and pats your knee with a reassuring hand. The motion crushes some of the stone on your knee, and a fine dust floats to the ground. A small part of you is surprised this doesn't hurt.

"Don't worry," he encourages. "When they run, the excitement thrills us. Then we can move."

That would explain how they caught you, you suppose. So you wait for a runner. It occurs to you that maybe William will come looking— but you negate that thought. He said three days. He won't come looking. Instead, he'll return to the village and add your name to those lost to the Howling Maw.

Disappointment settles like a deep pain within your stomach.

You have to catch a runner. When you do, you'll tell him to pick Searcher. He must pick Searcher.

In the mean time, you wait and watch. Well, you watch when you can pull your eyes away from the starlight above. Most of the time you gaze at that twinkling light because there's just something about it that draws you.

But when a runner passes, you'll be ready, you assure yourself. It'll excite you into action, and then you'll have a human to bring back Merriam's Light.

In the meantime, though, you gaze at the stars and wait.

The End

You *are* searching for gold, and if you want to help the stone people out, Merriam's Light. Saying "Searcher," then, is the more accurate answer.

"Searcher," you say to the wall.

The image of a sword glows, and you shade your eyes against the sharp light.

"Welcome, Searcher," says the voice. "Prepare for what lies beyond."

Behind you, there's a loud, ground-shaking clang. A glance back confirms a gate now stands between you and the room full of stone people. You're stuck.

The sword and star wall shudders. There's a concussion in the floor, and the wall begins to lower, inch by slow inch.

Prepare? What does that mean? The wall glowed with a sword. You don't have a sword, and your knife isn't exactly long enough to suffice. You shove the torch into a wall bracket, and then you pull an arrow and ready your bow as the wall finishes disappearing. Beyond is a vaulted room with heavy pillars.

You sneeze with the dust now floating in the air from the wall's disturbance.

On the far side of the room is a raised platform with a statue of a woman, her head thrown back and arms outstretched in front of her. In her palms rests a large, multifaceted crystal, and at her feet sits an ornate chest so large you doubt your arms could span it.

Merriam's Light and Treasure?

You only have a moment to take the statue in as movement draws your eye. Between you and the statue coils a massive snake. Coil upon coil begin to slide against each other, filling the still air with a rasping hiss. The head rises up and wavers as though the beast is contemplating you. Those reptilian eyes constrict with intent.

Your fingers around the bow go cold and numb, and the first shot goes wide. The arrow pings off the pillar behind the snake's head.

You bolt to the right just as the snake rears and snaps forward. Its head crashes into the pillar you ducked behind only seconds before.

You swing around the pillar and snap a shot off while the serpent's disoriented. Before the arrow hits, you know your aim is good. Even better, the thud of it hitting home fills you with some relief. You peek and find the arrow's shaft sunk deep into the serpent's green and black scales.

The snake screams in an ear-shattering cry that bounces off the stone walls like an angry hornet. It thrashes at the arrow, unable to dislodge it.

Wind howls into the cavern, combining with the serpent's agony. It pushes and pulls at you until standing becomes difficult. You lean against the pillar to shoot again, but the wind throws the shot far wide.

You scramble for another arrow just as the snake's head crashes into your shoulder. The massive jaws snap, not onto your arms, but onto the end of your bow. With a vicious tug, the bow is ripped from your grasp.

The expression on the serpent's face reminds you, chillingly, of a triumphant grin. It rears for a killing strike.

You pull your knife and thrust up into the serpent's chin as it snaps for your head.

The world goes black, and the only sound comes from your breath heaving in and out of your throat. Although you can feel the weight of the serpent on your dagger, you cannot see it inches from your face.

Is it dead?

A glowing light fills the room at the far end. It's the crystal in the statue's hands giving off prisms of light, colored in reds and yellows.

In the glow, the dead eyes of the snake glisten dully.

You shudder as you pull your dagger free and clean it on your pant leg. Looking too long at the dead serpent might freeze you in terror at what just happened. To avoid that fate, you turn away and approach the statue.

The wooden chest at its feet is huge but unlocked. You throw back the lid to find not gold but three leather bags.

The first one contains a fistful of gold, more than you've seen in your whole life, and plenty to feed the village for the year. You pocket the bag.

The next one reflects the light of the crystal as soon as you pull it open. Inside sit five perfectly smooth gems ranging from blood red to deep azure blue. You pocket it as well.

The last bag reveals a tiny rolled scroll. The paper crackles as you open it.

Human flesh has prevailed. Borrow my light but, do not leave with it or you will become the next stargazer.

You look at the crystal in the statue's outstretched hands. You're hesitant to take it, but it provides the only light in the cavernous temple. With gentle fingers, you pry the crystal from the statue and look around for a way out.

At the far side of the temple, the tall entry with the gate stands open. You didn't hear it, but you were a little preoccupied.

When you enter the cavern of the stone men, you find it filled with the faint silvery glow of starlight filtering through the hole in the ceiling. You hold the crystal high to see better. Its multifaceted surface catches the starlight and scatters rainbows around the room.

A prism lands on the stone man nearest you. In a puff of dust, the stone disappears and you're staring at Lawrence, the tanner's son who vanished a few months before. More and more people change from stone to flesh as you move through the cavern until you're staring at strangers mixed in with people you know from the village.

After everyone is returned to their human form, you replace the crystal in the statue's outstretched hands, and you return to the village, both rich and a hero.

The End

You know nothing about the stone creatures. Never even heard of them before, and although they seem really slow, they also look incredibly strong. You don't even want to imagine what could happen if one of them catches you. Caution seems like the best option.

You start into the cavern, walking at an almost uncomfortably slow pace. Gravel crunches under your feet but, because of your hunting experience, the sound stays soft beneath the pliable soles of your shoes. A few of the stone faces turn and blink as though confused by this small creature in their midst. They stare and a few cock their heads to the side. You freeze, knowing stillness often times is better than speed when trying to go unnoticed. After a short time, the stone faces turn away, unbothered apparently by the torch in your hand.

The creatures rumble and shift, their heavy appendages grinding and trailing out small streams of the dust they create with their motion. All the while they whisper to each other with words you can't quite make out despite the deep tone of their voices.

About half way across the cavern, a stone man stands up right in front of you. Even with his slow motion, his arm brushes your shoulder.

You freeze again as the head grinds to the side. It looks at its hand with what you would guess is confusion but again this passes, and the creature turns away to sit with a different group.

You start forward again only once the stone man has completely settled with his new set of friends. Each step is painfully slow but finally you reach the tall entryway. When you move to step through, however, you meet resistance.

The air ripples like a curtain disturbed by the wind, and your torch snuffs out without warning. You toss it aside before pushing harder against the unseen resistance. The faint ripples become more pronounced. You can see the wall beyond, shadowed in darkness, but when you try to press even harder, the resistance becomes solid to your touch.

You start to look around for a lever or something to allow you to pass when a chuckle sounds softly behind your right shoulder.

You jump and look to find a hunched, green-skinned man who, despite his hunch, does not look old. In fact, he bears no wrinkles on his jade skin. He leans against the wall with casual comfort.

"Can't go through there unless the gazers bid it." He gestures at the hall beyond the entryway and the room full of stone people. It's an airy wave of long, slender fingers that encompasses everything. "Come this way, I'll get you past."

His next gesture indicates a small tunnel behind him that you didn't see before.

You hesitate.

The green man chuckles but keeps it low as he shoots a glance at the stone men. He pushes off the wall to stand upright, but even still, the hunch in his back does not go away.

"There's another way if you like," he whispers, leaning toward you like a conspirator, "up there." He points to a high ledge from which you can reach the hole in the cavern ceiling.

"You can climb those little steps there. Just be careful since they tend to ice over. Seen a man or two fall." He points at the floor near the wall where some grayish bones show amidst the loose rubble of rocks.

You gulp and look from the gray bones to the hole in the ceiling. There are indeed steps of a sort, but they're more just holes cut into the stone than actual footholds. And even where you stand, you can see the slight sheen of frost coating them.

So far you haven't found anything to indicate there is gold down here. It might be better to get out while you still can. You're a good climber but it's a long way to fall if you lose your grip.

On the other hand, you know nothing about the green man. He might help you escape the Howling Maw, or he might be leading you into a trap.

If you follow the green man, flip to page 121
If you climb the steps, flip to page 127

Those small steps in the stone are incredibly icy. The longer you look at them, the more hazards you notice in climbing them. In fact, you can make out icicles hanging from a few of the higher spots, and you don't want to chance a fall from there.

"Get me past the entry," you tell the man.

He grins the biggest smile you've ever seen, which shows he has blue teeth. Against the green of his skin, it's a sharp contrast.

"Right this way." He bows, and leads you into the tunnel behind him. "Name's Roderick," he introduces. "It's been a while since I've had someone trust me."

"Not going to eat me, are you?" you tease, half afraid he'll grin again and say yes.

But the look he gives you is horrified. "I'm green," he says, "not a monster."

You chuckle. The look on his face brings too much relief for you not to let it out in some way. Then curiosity overcomes you, and you ask, "Other than green, what are you?"

He sighs a gust of heavy breath. "I'm Merriam's ageless steward." He deepens his voice like it's a pronouncement. The moment passes, and his shoulders slump again. "Was a man once, but now I'm just me. Green, ageless, and stuck." He shoots you a look.

"What?" you ask.

"You're bolder than most," he answers and stops at the next intersection in the tunnel. "I'll make you a deal. Come back and talk with me from time to time, and in return, I'll show you the temple, including all the little hidey holes that contain valuables."

Considering he hasn't eaten you, his offer is a no-brainer. You came here in hopes of money for food. Plain and simple.

"Deal," you say.

You get that big, blue grin again.

Roderick touches a tiny spot in the wall that sticks out a bare millimeter from the rest of the stone. A tiny shelf opens to reveal a leather bag. He pulls it out and hands it over.

The bag clinks, and the weight of it makes you grin with excitement. Peeking inside, sure enough, you find gold. It's enough to get the village through the month, maybe longer. You've never seen so much of it in one place.

"This is too much," you protest.

Roderick holds up a long hand before you can move to give the bag back. "Means nothing to me down here. Someday maybe we'll attempt to free me, but that involves facing several basilisks. Not my idea of fun. For now, just visit me."

"All right," you agree, although you still feel like he just handed you the world.

Roderick nods and turns to lead you out through a tunnel. It opens into the forest where you were hunting earlier in the day. It's not the Howling Maw, for which you're grateful.

"Use this tunnel to visit me," Roderick advises. He hands over a key to the gate that closes the tunnel from the outside world.

It's a while before you go to find William where he waits for you. The shock on his face when he sees you is gratifying.

"How'd you escape? Did you find it? What's inside?" The questions roll out of him unconstrained, and you let them roll without attempting to answer.

Somehow you don't think Roderick wants the world to know of his existence. Plus, with the dangers you found and Roderick hinted at, you don't want to encourage others to enter the Maw.

By the time William calms enough for you to speak, you roll out as simple an answer as you can think of.

"Found a small tunnel and followed it," you say. "There were a lot of bones in it, and amidst them I found this small bag." You show him the bag of coins. "It's enough to feed us for awhile, so I figured that was good enough and I found my way out."

William stares at you for a moment, "What else?"

You shudder without meaning to. "Not worth speaking about," you say.

He nods, like that confirms his suspicions, and doesn't ask about the Maw again.

You return from time to time, without William, to visit Roderick, and he shows you new sections of the Maw while you talk.

He tells you about Merriam, the wizard who acts using wind and darkness. The room you could not enter, in fact, is the Temple of Night and Wind. He shows it to you from a peek hole in the temple's wall.

You see Merriam's statue holding a crystal, but you also see a gigantic snake, a basilisk, guarding it. You steer clear of it, hang out with Roderick, and help feed the village with the money from the temple.

The End

The green man shifts from foot to foot, apparently impatient for your answer. He's more disturbing than the room full of stone people. Nothing in your experience tells you how to react to a completely green, hunched man who came out of nowhere.

"I'll chance the steps," you tell him.

His face falls into a look of total rejection, and he acts like he wants to say more. Even though he opens his mouth no sound comes out. For a moment you reconsider, but you shake off the feeling and turn toward the steps.

You're a strong climber. You should be able to handle this.

At the bottom of the steps, you glance back to see the man watching you from his tunnel. His gaze is unnerving, but you determine to ignore him and stretch your fingers. You jump up and down a few times to get your blood fully flowing, and finally you approach the climb, totally focused on the task at hand.

Those steps are tiny, even when you're standing right in front of them. You kind of hoped they'd be bigger when you went to grasp ahold.

You begin to climb. Your fingers fit into the holes up to the second knuckle. Your feet, with your soft hunting shoes, slide in almost to the ball of your foot. On any other climb, such holds would be enough. Would be a luxury, in fact, and the first few steps aren't bad. The ice that coats them melts with your touch and, being careful, you find you can get a solid hold.

The cold of the stone, however, seeps into your skin with unrelenting force. It starts out as numbness in your fingers and expands as the wind pulls away the warmth even more.

As you move higher, the ice stops melting, partly because of its thickness, and partly because your hands no longer hold the warmth to melt them.

You get a firm grip on the next step with your left hand by forcing more than just your fingers into the hole. If you could feel it, you'd wince at the scraping of your flesh, but you can't feel it by now.

With a secure hold, you stuff your right hand into your pocket to warm it. Once it's sufficiently tingly warm, you switch your hands.

It's then that a gust of wind picks up to buffet your body. It pulls at you, and you have to grab tight with both hands. You make the mistake of glancing down. Dizziness swims in your head, and you swallow convulsively. You're higher than you realized.

A new gust of wind, strong and bitterly cold, catches you just as you're closing your eyes to regain your equilibrium. The wind pulls you away and, before you know it, you're falling.

Unfortunately the rest of your story is too sad to tell in detail. The green man, the steward of the temple, takes pity on you and doesn't leave your bones with the rest. Instead, he buries you and places a little marker at your grave saying,

Here lies a brave searcher from Merriam's Temple of Night and Wind.

The End

A shudder travels through your body at the whispering wind coming up the stairs on the left. Ghosts creep you out, and that moaning, murmuring breeze creates all sorts of ugly pictures in your mind about what you might find at the bottom.

You place your hand on the latch of the iron-banded door and slowly lift it. The metal grinds but, with the slow pressure of your hand, the sound stays soft enough to combine with the wind and not be heard over it.

The door swings open a crack, and you lean forward to peek into the room beyond. It sits empty despite the large fire dancing in the pit in the middle of the room. You watch the shadows flickering around the walls for a moment just to be sure, and then you step inside.

Half the room's ceiling has caved in, leaving a jumble of jagged rocks strewn about the floor, but the part undamaged by the cave-in holds two small stone tables against the left wall.

You move to the two tables and find a single book on each. Their dusty covers appear undisturbed for quite some time.

The first one is titled *Below the Cavern*. You shift to see the other and find it announces itself as *Through the Darkness*.

You open *Below the Cavern* and twitch, startled to find the picture on the first page looks exactly like the room in which you're standing. In fact, a figure stands at one of the small stone tables looking through the book atop it. That figure boasts the same build and hair as yourself. You swing around, but there's nothing behind you but the empty room and blazing fire.

Looking back at the book, the figure moves as you go to turn a page. You stick your elbow out. The picture does likewise. You bob your head back and forth and watch your double do the same. Only long years of hunting experience keeps you from bolting from the room.

Best course of action, you firmly remind your jangled nerves.

You lean in to look closer at the picture. It shows the cave-in and all its rubble, the two tables and their books, and even your back as you lean closer. But it also shows a tunnel on the far wall that you didn't notice before. A thin chain glows beside it, and you look up to locate what the volume says should exist. Sure enough, there's a chain on the far wall that you can see through the crackling fire.

With a deep breath, you thump the book closed and move to investigate *Through the Darkness* where it sits on its table. Dust poofs into the air as you flip the cover open.

The first page is the same room, figure, fire, cave-in, and all, except the angle is from your right instead of behind you. It reveals a door on the other side of the stone table at which you stand. A lever in the floor glows under the table.

This time you catch the words below the picture.

Through the darkness you may find a friend and gold, but only if you are bold beyond the dragon's breath.

Checking *Below the Cavern*, you find words there too.

Take a breath before you descend, there may be treasure on the other end, but only if you pass the wizard's bend.

You flip through both books to see what else they contain but find they mostly tell a history of something called The Temple of Night and Wind. A quick scan of the first page in each confirms it's a long, dry history that could take you a long time to read. You're not comfortable sitting down in the Howling Maw to read a book when anything could show up at any time to attack you. People haven't disappeared in the Maw because they died reading a history book. There's got to be something dangerous down here.

You read the words below each picture again and debate which way to go. They are so cryptic! Neither one really tells you what to expect through each door.

If you choose *Below the Cavern*, flip to page 137
If you choose *Through the Darkness*, flip to page 159

Take a breath before you descend, there may be treasure on the other end, but only if you pass the wizard's bend.

You're not thrilled with darkness, and treasure to pay for food is why you embarked on this adventure in the first place. You skim *Below the Cavern* once more, and tuck it into your pocket before approaching the small chain in the wall across the room.

A quick inspection does not turn up anything suspicious, so you pull the chain. The floor drops beneath you in a stomach-lurching moment of terror.

The fall is not far, but even still, you land with a thud and groan in pain. Your pride is more hurt than anything else, you realize, as you take stock of your body. Once you're sure nothing is seriously damaged, you look around the circular room you landed in.

Above you is a grate that closed behind your fall. Even if you could reach the ceiling and climb back up, the hole's covered.

Thankfully you're not in complete darkness due to a small tunnel that emits light to your left. It's a small opening, but it's the only option in the room. You take the bow off you shoulder and push it through ahead of you. Then you crawl in on your hands and knees, pushing the bow in front.

As you go, there's a tiny tunnel to your right. It's small enough that you're not sure your shoulders will fit through. You crawl past it.

The bow sticks out in front of you as you proceed, and it's the first thing to leave the other end of the tunnel a few moments later. There's a bright flash and the bow bursts into flame, turning to cinders in the matter of a few seconds.

You yelp and shrink back, barely missing catching your sleeves on fire too.

You wait to see if anything else will happen. Nothing does. The shape of the bow lies on the floor in an outline of ash, warning you that something ahead could kill you, and quickly. You crawl forward to peek into the hallway beyond your little tunnel.

The corridor T's with your tunnel. To the left it goes a short ways and ends in a pile of stone. To the right is a long hallway with a statue of a tall woman, her head thrown back and arms outstretched in front of her. In her upturned palms rests a large crystal.

Light from somewhere above hits the crystal, and it fractures into thousands of tiny prisms scattered across the floor. The end of what's left of your bow rests under one of those prisms.

Testing, you slide the tip of an arrow

under that rainbow of light. In a flash it catches and burns to nothing but ash.

The hall's littered with the tiny prisms.

The end of the corridor with the rubble has a small gap above it, but it's far too narrow for you to slip through, and the size of the rubble makes moving it unlikely.

Behind the statue, you can see more corridor and what looks like a way out. But you have to get there first. The amount of ash on the floor hints you're not the only one to attempt such a feat.

As you look around, a small chain catches your eye on your right. It's tiny and only a thorough inspection would reveal it. Etched in letters just as small as the chain are the words "Take a breath…" and below that is a sketch of a waterfall.

You could pull the chain, but a waterfall in such a tight space could drown you just as easily as it could disable the crystal and its mass of prisms. If the whole corridor fills with water, you're not sure you can swim to the other end of the corridor in time to get out.

Or you could use your hunting knife to deflect the prism light and make your way slowly past the statue. It'd be a tight fit, though, and you'd have to be precise with each motion of your body and dagger.

You glance back at the tunnel you came

down. Perhaps that tiny tunnel doesn't look too small after all. The possibility of getting stuck in it fills you with dread, but is it worse than bursting into flames? You're not sure.

If you pull the chain, flip to page 143
If you use your dagger, flip to page 149
If you squeeze into the tiny tunnel, flip to page 91

You're not sure there's enough space to navigate between the prisms even if you deflect the light with your knife. You're not even sure the knife won't melt if you try it.

Plus, the inscription echoes the book. It's got to be connected, and although it tricked you once already, it didn't kill you.

You crawl into the corridor and suck yourself tight against the wall to avoid the prisms. Taking a deep breath, you reach down and pull the chain.

There's a rushing like the river in the spring thaw. Through and over the rubble to your left, water rushes into the corridor in a torrent of froth and motion.

It sweeps your feet away and whirls you around in its current. Before you know it, the corridor's full, and the water's no longer moving. The breath you took has seeped out as the water buffeted your body, and your chest already aches with the need to breathe again.

Your vision sparks around the edges as you try to swim. Your chest spasms, trying to pull breath against the better judgment of your brain. Your swimming grows weak, and you're not even sure you're swimming in the right direction.

You're about to drown.

There's a concussion to the water, a release like a dam breaking. The water starts to move again, then gushes, pulling you with it.

You smack into the statue and are past it so fast you can't grab ahold. The water swirls you around a corner. It dumps into a square room with a clatter. The water drains through a grate in the floor, and a few flashes of gold disappear with it.

Sputtering and coughing, you pull in a beautiful breath of air. Instantly the ache in your body subsides, and you rise to your hands and knees. Beneath you, around you, beyond your sight, are piles of gold coins.

You roll to sit and burst out laughing. It's filled with joy and relief and serves as a release for your pent-up, stretched-raw nerves. You haven't made it out yet, but you found gold, and that is half of your quest.

Once you recover your breath enough to stand, you locate a small satchel in a corner and fill it with the coins.

Then you look around for a way out. There's only one door that you can find but as you prepare to leave, you're thrown back and a voice states, "You cannot leave the Temple of Night and Wind with the instructions."

The book in your pocket grows uncomfortably warm. You use your sleeve to protect your skin as you pull it out. A wind kicks up and lifts the book from your hands. In a flash, the room goes dark, and after a brief moment of intense wind, the torches flare to life again. The book's gone.

The wind stills to unnatural calm. This place is the oddest experience of your life. You'll be glad to put it behind you. Attempting the door again, you're able to pass.

You follow the hallway beyond, and it dumps you back into the circular room with the fire. You look at the door and shake your head. It's the one the book originally showed you. The book itself is back on its table.

At least you know how to get out from here. The hallway from the treasure room closes as you enter the room. Once it's fully closed, the door fades, and you're looking at a stone wall. If you ever want to return for more treasure, you realize, you will have to brave the flood again. You shudder.

The look on William's face when you emerge from the Howling Maw gives you a chuckle. He clearly did not expect to see you again. He asks a lot of questions at first, but finding you unwilling to answer, he finally lets it go. None of the villagers ask either. You become the village hero but are viewed with some apprehension.

Everyone wonders what happened within the Howling Maw, and so, as time goes on, the villagers start to view you as not completely human. You let them believe what they will because you don't wish anyone else the adventure of the Maw.

The End

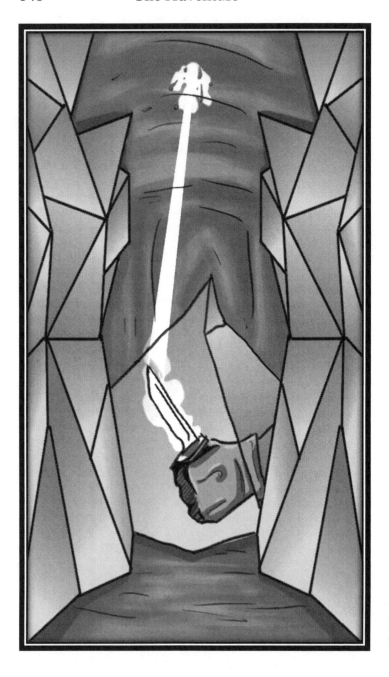

The book tricked you once. You're hesitant to follow its leading again. You ignore the chain with the inscription and instead crawl with great care out of the tunnel.

You draw your hunting knife with its six-inch blade and hold it in front of the first prism. It deflects the light with a popping sound and, where it hits the ceiling, it sparks and drops chucks of stone onto the floor. You're suddenly very thankful the prism didn't melt the knife in your hand.

You step past where the deflected prism usually hits the floor into a narrow, clear space beyond it, and with careful precision, you move the knife to the next prism. The original rainbow of light hits the floor mere inches from your feet.

Again there's a popping, and stone explodes as the next prism hits a new spot on the ceiling. It kicks up dust that you inhale before you can hold your breath. A cough catches you, and your hand jerks. You freeze, fighting the need to cough again and swallowing until the urge goes away.

There's a familiar shake in your hands now. You've experienced the sensation while hunting after a sudden spike of excitement or fear, and you wait for that uncontrollable tremor to pass before sliding past the next prism and moving on.

You make your way down the corridor in this fashion until you're even with the statue. It feels like ages have passed, but really the process has only taken perhaps half an hour. When you move to step beyond the statue, you meet resistance. The air shimmers like a curtain disturbed by the wind.

"Only the deluge passes the bend," a voice states.

"What?" you ask, but there's no answer except for the book in your pocket growing warm. The crystal in the statue's hands glows brighter, which intensifies the light of the prisms.

Unnerved, you try to step forward again. This time it doesn't resist you. Instead, it captures you, freezing you in place with one foot a few inches off the ground.

The statue pivots to face you, bringing the crystal with it. Dozens of prisms glide across the floor and walls with popping stone following in its wake until the sweep of the light lands on you. You flinch as dozens of prisms touch your body.

Nothing happens.

"See what you almost achieved and then be expelled," the voice says.

Expelled? That does not sound good, but you still can't move even as your legs begin to shake.

The statue continues to pivot until it faces down the corridor where you were heading. The crystal's light narrows into a focused beam and shines into a room at the far end of the corridor. Gold glints like dozens of eyes. That room beyond is filled with the very thing you were hoping to find.

A stone slab slams shut on that room as you give a cry of dismay. A heavy wind kicks up, and it surrounds you like a giant hand. Your stomach sinks as you realize the wind is lifting you off the floor and toward a small hole in the ceiling. It's this hole, you see, that lets in light to touch the crystal, but it's tiny. A cat might fit through, but definitely not a person.

As you watch the ceiling draw closer, sure you're about to be squished against the stone, that hole expands. At first it's large enough for a cat and eventually maybe a medium sized dog, until it finally reaches a size where you're no longer worried about slamming into the ceiling.

You find yourself dumped on the forest floor where you were hunting earlier in the day. The wind continues to howl out of the hole, throwing you backward. As you stumble, the book, *Below the Cavern,* falls from your pocket.

Like a greedy child, the wind picks up the book and carries it back into the ground. With a thwamping sound, the hole vanishes behind it, and you're left alone in the eerie silence of the forest.

You were so close! You push off the ground and move to find the Howling Maw again. You stop. This is part of the danger of the Howling Maw, you realize. It enthralls you with the desire to win and come away with the gold. It teases you with the sight to trick you to try again.

You sigh out your frustration and head toward the Howling Maw, but only to find William. You might attempt the Maw again at another time, but if you do, you'll go in better prepared. For now, you need to find your friend and head back to the village to find a new bow.

The End

Questions spin through your head until you feel dizzy. The stone people didn't tell you much to go on, and you're not even sure you trust them.

"A moment to consider, please," you say to the wall.

The sword and star disappear in a flash of raw red light. Immediately after, the entire slab of stone throbs red.

"Time is not an option," the wall says.

The floor drops from under your feet and your stomach lodges in your throat. The throbbing red of the wall seems to have been imprinted on your eyes because that is all you can see in the darkness that now surrounds you.

You land with a smack against a cold stone floor and simply lay still as your body reports its multiple pains. You find your bow still slung over your shoulder, amazingly unbroken. Your knife rests reassuringly in its sheath. The now lifeless torch rolls away on the floor.

You're not left to recover in peace. There's a fluttering sound in the darkness like the pages of a book being ruffled by a breeze. A cool wind brushes your skin, bringing goose flesh to your arms.

Faint red light glows, hovering a few feet from your face. You blink to focus and realize you're looking at words on a page.

Through the darkness you may find a friend and gold, but only if you are bold beyond the dragon's breath.

You grasp the edges of the book and it comes to rest fully in your hands. The feel of its dusty cover brings you back to where you lie. You can't lie on the floor forever.

Pocketing the volume, you push to your feet and decide you have to continue on. Even with your drop through the floor and your protesting body, you seem just as unbroken as your bow. It might be a small miracle.

You find the wall with your hand and rest your palm against the cool surface until you feel steady enough to walk. Your first few steps are shaky, but you realize it's as much from the floor as your lack of balance.

Flip to page 160 to continue

Through the darkness you may find friend and gold, but only if you are bold beyond the dragon's breath.

Below the Cavern makes your skin crawl with its talk of holding your breath. On the other hand, darkness doesn't really bother you. You pocket *Through the Darkness* and pull the lever under the table.

As the picture depicted, a door opens, releasing a gust of chilly air. A thrill of excitement fills you. So far, this is proving to be rather fun with secret passageways and all. You pull a torch from the wall and enter the door with a light step.

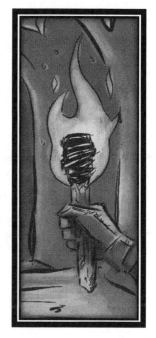

The door slams shut and the torch goes out with a puff. Darkness descends like a heavy blanket to surround you. So the book was serious about the darkness.

Great.

You drop the now useless torch and place your palm against the cool wall. The texture beneath your touch feels gritty like a place untouched in ages.

The floor under your feet slopes drunkenly left and right in great waves. You're glad for the wall since it feels like you're rising and falling over a series of washboards. As you step forward, however, it's clear you're still moving straight despite the floor's unevenness. It's a reassuring thing to know you're making progress even if the destination is unknown.

Wind howls softly past, chilling your face and making your fingers numb around the wood of your bow. The howl of the wind is a constant, low sound that brings a slight ringing to your ears. You flex your fingers to keep blood flowing in them and shake your head to shrug off the low howl.

With a tight grip on your bow, you keep moving over the uneven floor.

There's a puff of very warm air. It's sudden with its sharp contrast to the cool wind. Your excitement for this venture drains away as every nerve in your body warns you to run.

Your hunting experience, however, makes you pause instead of bolting and possibly running into an unseen obstacle. Many creatures are more likely to attack an animal that bolts, and you want to not be prey for as long as possible. That puff of hot air doesn't repeat as you stand still. You start forward again, and a puff of hot air hits your face a second time.

It's filled with the stench of rotten meat.

You freeze and tilt your head upward to look. Everything is still blanketed in darkness and so when you spot them, they stand out with deadly intent lit by the life behind them.

The wide-spaced, slitted eyes of a reptile glow back at you. Terror tightens in your chest. Considering the spacing of those eyes, the creature must be quite the giant. You release the grip on your bow and reach for your knife since the creature's too close for you to get a shot off. All the while you keep your gaze fixed on those reptile eyes above you.

"No, no," whispers a voice that is far too close to be comforting, "keep walking."

You hesitate.

Keep walking?

"Be bold *beyond* the dragon's breath, not under it! Keep walking."

_____

If you keep walking, flip to page 163
If you attack with your knife, flip to page 169

The voice quotes the book, which hasn't led you wrong yet. With numb fingers, you sheath the knife. Then, because you can't move forward without feeling like you have some way to defend yourself, you pull an arrow and ready it. Satisfied, you start walking again.

Those yellow eyes follow you with great puffs of hot air across your face. The stench of it fills your nose, and you swallow hard, both in fear and revulsion.

"Smart," says the voice. "When I tell you to, shoot *directly* between the eyes."

Your hands shake but you keep moving across the uneven floor. Instead of taking tall steps, you glide the soles of your feet over the stone. If you find something on the floor, you have no desire to fall over it. This way, your feet will touch anything in the way long before you kick or stumble over it.

The creature gives a low hiss, and more foul breath washes across your face.

"Almost," the voice says.

The eyes blink in a lazy fashion, and more hot breath rolls forth. A couple more steps confirm your suspicion. The eyes have stopped moving along with you.

"Now!"

You raise the bow and shoot in one smooth motion. There's a deep thud that in the stillness of the tunnel sounds final. The eyes blink and disappear with a softer thud.

The hall floods with light and you jump.

Beside you stands a hunched green man who, despite his hunch, does not look old.

"Spectacular!" he exclaims, jumping up and down in glee. "No one's trusted me like that before." He points up to emphasize his comment.

You look at where you last saw the eyes and see, instead of a stone ceiling, a glass cage containing the body of a giant serpent. The great creature couldn't get to you, you realize.

Its blood drips around the arrow protruding from between its eyes. Where the fluid falls to the glass, it sizzles, creating the light that now fills the hall. As you study the cage, you locate what you're looking for. Tiny holes line the bottom. Through these you felt the serpent's breath as you walked below it, but they're too small for an arrow. The last hole in the cage is bigger, however. It's not by much, but it's enough for your shot to hit and kill the serpent.

"Why didn't you tell me?" you ask.

"I've told others. None listened." He shrugs. "Name's Roderick." He sticks out a hand and you shake, telling him your name.

"Follow me." He turns on a heel and runs down the hall in excitement. He stops at a small door on the right-hand side and opens it.

The space beyond is no bigger than a closet but on the floor sits a chest. You glance at him and, at his nod, lift the lid to find the glitter of coins.

Relief floods you. There's plenty to feed the village for years to come.

"I can't carry it all," you mumble in dismay.

"Then don't." Roderick holds out a small satchel. "Take some and come back. I'd love the company. Just don't tell people. They tend to die when they venture into the temple."

"Thank you," you say and take the bag. After filling it, you sling it across your shoulder, and Roderick leads you out.

"You can get back in this way to visit me," he says and hands you a small key to the door. It leads you out into the forest under the exposed roots of a tree. As you walk away, Roderick waves with a giant grin on his face. You realize he's got blue teeth that stand out sharply against his green skin.

You retrieve William, who still waits for you at the entrance to the Howling Maw. Between the two of you, you come up with a story about a distant uncle dying and leaving you a small fortune.

Neither one of you wants people to wander into the Maw for the fun of it. William himself, after hearing your story, promises not to enter the Maw either. He wants nothing to do with a green man or giant snake.

Even with the story, however, you're careful when you return to the Maw. Roderick gives you a big blue-toothed grin, and you're glad you trusted him. He becomes a friend you can rely on for life.

The End

The creature stares with unblinking yellow eyes. Its breath wafts over you in waves of foul stench. Even though you can't see your knife or your hand, you feel the fine tremors in your limbs that prevent you from holding the weapon steady. Your nerves can't handle walking under the creature now staring at you.

In a decisive motion, you jab at the thing right between the eyes with a yell.

There's a chunk! And the knife stops dead before hitting home. A cracking like ice over a pond fills the tunnel. With a sharp ping, the ceiling rains down in shards. You shield your face with an arm, and the falling debris scratches at your skin.

"Run!" shouts the voice.

You don't need to be told twice.

You take off down the hall, stumbling right and left as the uneven floor catches at your feet. Faint light appears ahead. You aim for it just as you hear a deep hissing in the tunnel. Something scratches the floor, making you picture giant claws digging grooves into the stone. From the sound of it, those claws drive the creature forward, and it's gaining speed.

"Leave the book!" shouts the voice. "You can't leave with it. Drop the book!"

The book, *Through the Darkness*, grows hot in your pocket. Scrambling for it, you finally pull it out and pitch it behind you. As you do, you spot those slitted eyes only a few feet away.

You press forward with added motivation, puffing breath in and out of your lungs. The light ahead clarifies into an opening with the forest beyond.

With a burst of speed, you shoot out into the forest and glance back as you continue running. A giant snake's head appears in the door and stops with a jerk.

The creature pulls back and strikes forward again but is pulled up short by some invisible force. It screams an ear-stinging scream that has you whimpering for it to stop. The door closes, cutting off that painful sound and forcing the snake to retreat. The door disappears, and where it stood a boulder now stands in its place.

You stop, huffing, and place your hands on your knees to catch your breath. William is never going to believe this. After you calm your breath, you go to retrieve him and return home, empty handed but alive.

The End

The Adventure
of
<u>The Tournament</u>
By Jennifer M Zeiger

Illustrated
By
Joseph Apolinar

Rain drips from the porch above, and the siding of the building weeps with moisture. For the moment, though, you're dry. Your small, sheltered spot is just a protected piece of cobblestone. It's a two-foot by two-foot section where the rain isn't drenching the ground. There's not even enough space to lie down, but the spot's yours, and as long as you don't move from it, no one will challenge you.

You're not homeless. You just can't find an inn that's not already full because of the tournament being held at the coliseum. Considering the situation, you may as well be homeless, but at least you're a well-armed homeless.

Thus why no one will challenge you for your shelter.

A sword peeks over your right shoulder from its scabbard on your back. From your belt hangs a woodsman's knife the length of your forearm, and in your right hand you hold an unstrung bow. Over your left shoulder, the fletching of your arrows plays peek-a-boo around the hood of your dark cloak.

All of the weaponry right now is just extra weight. Your cloak is the prize possession with the rain. Its wool weight settles around you with delicious warmth as its outer layer beads the bit of rain that reaches you under the porch.

You sigh, reminding yourself that you're putting up with this for a reason. The tournament boasts a number of challenges including fencing, archery, jousting, and hand-to-hand combat. They all pay well for each winner.

You're not here for the pay, though. You're here for a person. You've heard nothing from your family since you chose to be a woods ranger instead of a baker like the rest of them.

But a few days ago a messenger found you where you were hunting in the forests to the north. He settled on the ground opposite your campfire and warmed his chilled fingers as he passed along the message your family sent with him.

"King's men took your Uncle Ruben," he said, "because your family can't pay the rent on the bakery. He's been sentenced to working the quarry until he pays off the amount due."

"What do they want from me?" you asked, perplexed. You passed across the fire a mug of warm tea to help the messenger fight off the night's chill.

You've got no influence in the King's justice system, despite being one of his rangers. Working the quarry is hard, dangerous work, you know, but the bakery's debt can't be *that* high. Ruben shouldn't be there that long.

The messenger sipped several times before continuing his message. You wondered how long he'd been searching for you.

"The family hasn't paid in well over a year," the messenger finally explained, giving you a sheepish look. It's probably the same look your family gave while telling him, a complete stranger, their issue. "Ruben's assigned the quarry for the next five years to pay everything off."

Dread settled a heavy stone into your stomach. No one survived the quarry that long.

"All right," you conceded, "what does the family want?"

"In the King's tournament, you can ask for the release of a worker if you win one of the challenges." As he said this, the man eyed your bow where it sat against a nearby tree and the sword laying on the ground beside your knee.

You had an "ah-ha" moment. No one in the family could win such a challenge—except you. You considered refusing. The family hasn't spoken to you in years, much less lent a hand whenever you needed something, but this was about a man's life, family or not.

"When does the tournament start?" you asked.

"Beginning of the week." Again, that sheepish look came over his face.

And now you're hunkered under a porch

instead of sleeping in an inn because, by the time the messenger found you, you only had two days to get to the capital.

An inn wouldn't have helped much anyway, you tell yourself. There's only an hour or two before sunrise, at which time you have to be at the coliseum to check in as a contestant.

As you wait for the warmth to arrive from the rising sun, you debate whether to try archery or fencing. You've never attempted jousting and don't want to start now. As a last resort you can try hand-to-hand combat, but that's not your forte, and you'd prefer to start with your stronger skills.

If you pick Archery, go to page 181
If you pick Fencing, go to page 187

The rain subsided with the morning sun, and now you stand in line to register for the King's tournament with the daylight warming your shoulders. The mists have long since burned off, leaving a crisp chill to the air. Your cloak is almost dry as you approach the wooden table at the entrance to the coliseum.

The man behind the table holds his pen over a sheet of paper. Without looking up, he waits for you to say which challenge you want to participate in.

"Archery," you inform him.

He grunts and accepts the papers you hold out containing your information. They tell him everything from your name, to where you were born, to which family you belong, and what profession they claim. They don't, however, tell him a thing about what you've done since being born. Nowhere on the papers does it state your personal profession.

"A baking family?" he asks, finally looking up and pointing at your last name.

"Mostly," you reply. It comes out clipped, which wasn't your intention, but you've been questioned like that your whole life.

He eyes you and your weaponry and shrugs before handing your papers back.

"The Archery field's to the left," he says.

"First tournament starts in an hour."

You thank him and move on.

The coliseum's huge, made to support gaming events and trials, but today, instead of hosting a single event, the ground is split into five wedges like a pie. Spectators mill around the seating above, able to see all five arenas from where they stand.

On the ground, however, you can only see the wedge you're standing in and the two neighboring wedges to the right and left.

Once you're in the archery wedge, you can see the hand-to-hand arena on the far side. Closer, on the near side, you make out the fencing grounds. You guess jousting is on the other side of the coliseum because several horse heads stand out above the human crowd in that direction.

The fifth wedge you can't guess at. All you can see in that area is a crowd milling about.

You approach the table at the edge of the archery field and hold out your papers to the man standing behind it. He waves the papers away and points to a spot on the ground.

"Stand there and wait," he grumbles.

Where he pointed is a spot in the middle of the wedge but closer to the narrow side of the pie. You move to it and nod at the man beside you. He's standing in place as well and behind him stand five others, all holding bows. They are your competition.

The man sneers but the look vanishes as you pull your bow from your back, step through and into it, and string the long bow in one fluid motion. This is your comfort zone. As a ranger, you're not only required to hunt and keep the forests clear of dangerous animals, but you're required to train for long shots in case of war. You're the snipers of the kingdom, as it were. A little known fact, but you don't explain this to the man.

Instead, you pull your cloak off, slide your arrows back over your shoulder, and pull on the bow a little to feel the draw. You nod at the man again and turn to face the field where several targets are placed.

The first one's close, about a hundred yards out. If you're not careful, you'll put an arrow all the way through the target at that range. The second target's another fifty yards or so, and the third doubles the first. A 200-yard shot. Now that's where your bow will give you the advantage.

This first round must be designed to weed out the amateurs. You jump up and down to warm your body while waiting.

Finally, the man from the table walks out onto the field and raises his hands for attention.

The archery wedge goes silent.

"First round," he shouts in a voice that bellows through the coliseum. "Three targets each. Hit the bull's eye on the targets. Top four contestants will proceed to the next round. We start with the archer on that end." He points to the man on your left and then leaves the field.

Once he's clear, he gives a nod to the first archer. The man takes aim, and his three arrows hit within an inch of the bulls' eyes in rapid succession.

Your turn. After pulling out an arrow, you hold it loosely against the string while you eye the first target. You wait for the noise and motion around you to fade. Nerves make your hands sweat. You wipe them on your pants without looking away from the target.

Your ears ring with silence. Your peripheral vision becomes nothing but gray. The muscles in your back tighten, and the bow comes up in one move.

Then the arrow's away, and you're pulling the second before the first hits its mark. By the time you release the third arrow, the dull thud of the first has already sounded, and the second follows immediately after.

You know as soon as you release the first that it was off but, when you look back, it sits right beside the arrow of the man who shot first. Your other two are dead center of the targets.

You find yourself almost holding your breath as the others go, hoping your initial mistake doesn't ruin your shot at the top four archers. The last man shoots, and you breathe out in a heavy sigh. You made it to the next round.

The announcer points to you and the other three who passed the first challenge. You all step forward.

He points at you again. "Distance or Difficulty?" he shouts. The question bounces around while he awaits your answer.

If you choose Distance, go to page 227
If you choose Difficulty, go to page 245

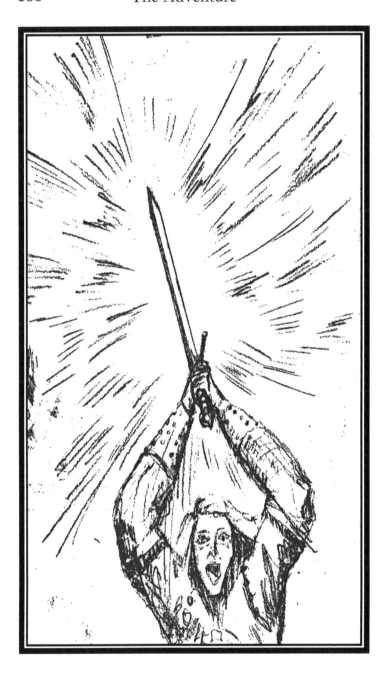

The rain subsided with the morning sun, and now you stand in line to register for the tournaments with the daylight warming your shoulders. The mists have long since burned off, leaving the air with a crisp chill. Your cloak is almost dry as you approach the wooden table at the entrance to the coliseum.

The man behind the table holds his pen over a sheet of paper. Without looking up, he waits for you to say which challenge you want to participate in.

"Fencing," you inform him.

He grunts and accepts the papers you hold out containing your information. They tell him everything from your name, to where you were born, to which family you belong, and what profession they claim. They don't, however, tell him a thing about what you've done since being born. Nowhere on the papers does it state your personal profession.

"A baking family?" he asks, finally looking up and pointing at your last name.

"Mostly," you reply. It comes out clipped, which wasn't your intention, but you've been questioned like that your whole life.

He eyes you and your weaponry and shrugs before handing your papers back.

"The fencing field's to the left past the

archery section," he says. "First tournament starts in an hour."

You thank him and move on.

The coliseum's huge, made to support gaming events and trials but today, instead of hosting a single event, the ground is split into five wedges like a pie. Spectators mill around the seating above, able to see all five arenas from where they stand.

On the ground, however, you can only see the wedge you're standing in and the two neighboring wedges.

Archery is immediately to your left, and beyond it you can see the fencing square. To your immediate right sits the hand-to-hand combat arena, and you guess jousting is on the other side of the coliseum because you can make out the heads of several horses in that direction.

The fifth wedge you can't guess at. All you can see in that area is a crowd milling about.

You pass through the archery wedge and make your way to the table in the fencing wedge. You hold out your papers to the man standing behind it. He grabs them from your hand and holds them directly in front of his watery eyes.

He snorts. "Baker? They'll let anyone in these days." He tosses the stack of papers onto his table and points to the palisade for the fencing square. "Stand in line. Your turn will come soon."

His attitude stiffens your spine, but you hold your tongue. People always comment on your family heritage. You've found the only way to silence such ridiculous assumptions is to show them you're a capable ranger.

You move to stand beside a man twice your height. He's broad enough to shoulder a wagon. He glances over and raises a brow.

"Speed?" he guesses.

"Perhaps," you admit. "Power?" You gesture at the broadsword he's carrying over his shoulder.

A toothy grin splits his face and he shrugs his broad shoulders. "Perhaps."

You grin back as you set the rest of your weaponry against the side of the fencing ring. You won't need the bow and arrows, and they might get in your way.

"First contestant," shouts a man standing at the opposite side of the square. "Obstacle or Multiple?"

"What's that mean?" asks the huge man.

It's your turn to shrug. "Guess we'll see."

The first man shuffles from one foot to the other, and finally blurts out, "Multiple."

The announcer gestures him into the ring, and then he gestures at the big man beside you, at you, and the woman behind you.

"Multiple contestants it is!" the announcer shouts as you all move into the ring.

It's not a lot of space for four people swinging swords.

"You must overcome two of the three others in the ring," the announcer explains. "If you step out of the ring, you're done. If you're struck down by one of your opponents, you're done. Good luck, Contestants."

Your stomach tightens into a heavy ball of nerves. They didn't blunt your swords for the challenge and the rules stated nothing about not killing.

"Work with me?" the big man asks out of the side of his mouth.

You know nothing about him. He could turn on you without warning. On the other hand, someone watching your back could be a huge asset.

_____

If you work with the man, go to page 193
If you go it alone, go to page 211

Considering your odds, you'd rather have someone on your side in this contest. You nod to the man in agreement.

He smiles and turns to square off against the other man in the ring. This move turns his back to you in a show of trust that's startling.

The woman contestant smirks and moves like she's going to surprise your partner from the side. After his show of trust, you're not about to let this woman catch him unawares. You move to put yourself between her and the big man.

You wait for the fencing match to begin. It's a moment, brief but heavy on the nerves, in which you eye each other, gauging your opponent's stance and weaponry.

"All right contestants." The announcer stands on the corner of the fencing ring to be seen above the crowd. "Remember, you must overcome two of the other three in the ring. NOW GO!"

His shout catches you all by surprise, and there's a pause of uncertainty. Usually they'd throw a flag to start a match, but apparently they planned these tournaments to be unorthodox. Everyone explodes into motion.

The woman's fast. You duck her first swing and catch her return swing on your sword. The clash of steel on steel sends a shock into your hands and up into your shoulders. She threw a lot of weight into the move, trying to force you off balance, even if she doesn't break through your block.

You shove her away and take a step back to rebalance. She regains her own center of gravity and circles, gauging you.

The crowd roars. It's deafening in the way a trumpet makes your ears ring.

You go on the offense and beat the woman back several steps with a series of blows that does not allow her to recover, only respond.

There's a deep-throated scream behind you that sends chills down your spine. It's your partner's voice, you're sure of it, but you don't chance a look as the woman tries to use the moment to her advantage. She swings and steps closer, trying to get within your longer reach.

You fast step out of her way and reverse your motion the instant her swing goes past. Before she knows it, you're beating her back again.

You've no desire to actually harm her, but judging from your partner's scream, no gentle hit will end the contest. The announcer said *overcome* two of the three in the ring. So it's knock her out or force her from the ring.

The fence around the ring sits just above her hips. To force her over that top rung will require some extra momentum, but the longer you fight her, the more you're convinced that it's your only option. At no time in the fight have you seen a chance to knock her unconscious. She's just too careful about her head.

With grim determination, you look for an opening to force her out of the ring. Your chance comes when she stumbles in an effort to side step. She keeps her sword up, but you push it slightly to the side with your own blade, step in close by taking three quick, almost running steps, and throw your shoulder into her sternum. You lift with your legs as you keep moving forward.

A huff of air escapes her, maybe from surprise or maybe from the force of your shoulder in her stomach, but then the backs of her knees hit the fence. She flies over the top rail while her sword hits the fence and tears from her grip. It clatters against the ground a second before the woman lands with a thud.

The spectators scream approval of your tactics.

Your stomach rolls as the woman's head hits the ground. You wait, but she doesn't move. A man checks her and gives you a thumbs up. She's unconscious.

Only then do you turn to see what's happening with the other two.

Your partner's right arm drips blood in a steady stream from a slice across his bicep. He struggles to keep his broadsword up as he blocks a strike from his opponent.

He pushes the smaller man away and attempts a swing. His movement is too slow, and the other man ducks inside his reach for a killing blow. The smaller man isn't going to pull short. His face scrunches in determination, and the muscles along his back and neck tense in total abandonment to his course of action.

You switch your grip on your own sword, rear back, and throw. At any sort of distance the throw would not be effective, but the fencing ring's small. The sword flies through the air and lands with a heavy thump with its hilt against the smaller man's temple.

There's a long pause of shock from everyone, and the man crumples in a boneless heap.

The crowd rises in ecstatic joy, roaring in excitement. Your ears ring as you join the big man and check on his bleeding arm. Tearing the sleeve from his shirt, you tie it around the wound.

"This isn't fencing," you grumble as you work. "This is butchery."

"Yeah," the big man agrees. "Thanks for the save."

Before you can respond, the announcer

steps up onto the corner of the ring and raises his hands for attention.

"Well done!" he shouts. "Now, since you obviously worked together, you can pick between Obstacles or Mastery." He holds out his hands for your choice.

You glance at the big man. He shrugs. Neither one of you have any clue what those options mean. His face is drawn with pain and you know, whatever you pick, it'll hurt him even more.

Could you possibly offer to compete for the both of you? It's a risky choice. People have been disqualified from tournaments before for trying to change the options.

If you choose Obstacles, go to page 199
If you choose Mastery, go to page 205
If you offer to compete for the both of you, go to page 259

Your partner's arm has bled through the bandage as you considered your options. If Mastery is a test of his swordsmanship, he won't do well. You're not sure what Obstacles means, but it'll at least give the man a chance with his wound.

"Obstacles," you tell the announcer.

"Obstacles it is!" he shouts and waves for several men standing beside the ring to prepare things.

They haul two heavy wooden boxes into the fencing ring and set them in the corner. A man stands on top of the boxes and waits to be told when to open them.

"What do you think is in them?" the big man asks.

You shrug, but there's a skittering coming from inside that makes your skin crawl into goose flesh.

"The goal," the announcer shouts above the general noise of the crowd, "is for our two contestants to fence with each other. Three strikes wins. But they must deal with the rats while they fight."

"Rats?" the big man grumbles. His brows draw into a deep frown, and he sounds exactly as you feel. Rats. Of all things, they had to pick rats.

You help the man to his feet, and you

each take an opposite corner. This time the announcer drops a flag. You wait for the white square of cloth to float to the ground.

Although your focus stays on the big man and his heavy sword, you hear the scrape of wood on wood as they release the rats into the ring.

At first you think the scheme unrealistic. What's to keep the little beasts from simply escaping the ring? But the rodents don't head for the crowd. Instead, they race around the wooden fence several times before heading straight for you and the big man. They've been trained for this. Great.

The big man takes two steps and is within range to swing. When you take the strike on your sword, your hands go numb. You're in trouble. Although you can't feel your hands now, you can feel the rats trying to climb into your pant legs.

They swarm over his legs as well but he's got high boots, and his pants are tucked snugly into the tops. Although the rats try to pull at the fabric, they make no progress in getting to his legs.

You manage to duck around him on the next attack and tap him on the side.

"Strike one!" the announcer shouts.

The big man grunts and comes at you again. You almost drop your sword with his strike. The longer you fence, the more the rats worm their way up your pant legs, and the less you can feel your hands and shoulders. One rodent makes its way to your knee and latches onto the skin at the back of your leg.

You kick in an effort to break him loose, but all this does is set you off balance. The big man takes the advantage by taking a note from your own book. As you stumble, he rushes in and shoves one heavy shoulder into your stomach.

Before you can react, he lifts and you sail backward in the air. Your heels clip the top of the fence, but there's no way to stop your backward motion.

"Sorry," he says as you land on your backside outside the ring. "Didn't want to hurt you."

You can't blame him. With his heavy sword, which they never blunted, simply striking without bruising or worse is quite difficult.

You nod and shake your leg hard to dislodge the rat still hanging onto your knee. The beast flies from the end of your pant leg, and you kick it back into the ring.

***

They line the contestants up in front of a pavilion once the day of contests is finished. You end up behind the big man as the second to win in the fencing matches.

The King steps forward to congratulate him. "What would you have as your prize?" he asks for all to hear.

"My daughter from the quarry," the big man answers.

You hold in a smile. Of all people to lose to, you couldn't have picked a better one. As he turns from the field, his eyes glisten with tears.

"Thank you," he whispers as he passes.

Those who came in second place are handed a small purse of coins. You pocket yours and head out to pay off a portion of Ruben's sentence with your prize. Once that's taken care of, you head back out to the woods.

It's not long after that another messenger finds you with a second message from the family.

"There's another tournament to the south," he explains. "The family would like you to compete again and use the purse to free Ruben."

The amount you paid already shortened Ruben's sentence by three years. Considering how the last tournament went, you tell the messenger the family can make their own contribution to Ruben's plight. The messenger leaves without comment, and you don't hear from the family again until years later, when Ruben tracks you down.

"Think I'm done with the bakery," he tells you. "The family made no effort other than contacting you to help me. Maybe I'll open my own shop."

He spends the night beside your fire and does indeed open his own shop, a confectionary, in the city.

The End

This tournament needs to end soon. Your partner's arm has bled through your makeshift bandage while you contemplated your options.

"Mastery," you say, hoping such a contest will move quickly.

"Mastery it is!" the announcer shouts for all to hear. He gestures at a man standing beside the ring, and the man hops the fence.

That motion alone tells you the Mastery contest is going to test your skills to the max. The man's well built but it's the way he moves that sends a knot straight into the pit of your stomach. It's like a cat walking along the top of a fence. Smooth and lithe without anything extra.

"We're in trouble," the big man mumbles.

"Yup," you agree.

"This is the King's Master Swordsman," the announcer tells the crowd. He turns to address you. "You both will fence with him at the same time. If you manage three hits on him between the two of you, you both win the fencing challenge. If, however, you fail and he wins three hits on either of you, then you walk away without any purse."

"I've heard rumors about this man," your partner says as you move to the corner opposite the Master. "Not sure he's ever been beaten."

"Great," you mutter. You both turn to face the man.

"And START!" the announcer shouts.

You move right, and your partner moves left. Before you get far, however, the Master closes on you and reigns a series of blows that you barely manage to keep from hitting home. By the time he backs off, you realize you've been maneuvered into the same corner as your partner.

The big man steps forward and swings his broadsword to give you a moment to recover. The Master changes his focus to take the broadsword. He doesn't catch the vicious swing head on. Instead he deflects it and spins around the big man, tapping him across the back as he goes.

"One hit for the Master!"

With his bleeding arm, getting three hits on your partner is going to be easy game for this expert swordsman. You step in to protect his side as he stumbles.

The Master gives you an appreciative grin and attacks again. You keep him away from your partner by simply backing away from him, but it's not long before you're stuck in another corner.

Your partner rushes in to help, and the

Master sneaks a tap under his broad swing.

You hold in a groan. The hit was on the same side as the bleeding arm. The big man crumples around that side, and you realize, too late, that his ribs must be bruised as well. The last hit comes before you can distract the Master from your wounded partner.

"Two and three!" the announcer shouts. "The Master has won again!"

The lithe swordsman bows and even that movement lacks any excess.

You sigh, accepting the outcome as inevitable.

***

"I'm sorry," the big man says again as you watch the winners of the tournament receive their purses from the King.

The Master swordsman doesn't even take a purse. He simply bows to the King and accepts a word of praise.

It rankles, but you shrug at the big man's apology. "Did the best we could."

"True, but my daughter's still in the quarry." You look over at the big man and see his shoulders are slumped forward and his head bowed.

"It won't free her immediately," you say, "but if you work with me in the Northern forest, help keep the villages free of wolves and bears, we can use the money to pay toward her debt."

His head swings up to look at you.

"You'd help me?"

You nod. "You watched my back today," you say. "It's been a long time since I could trust someone like that."

A slow smile pulls up the corners of his mouth.

And so your friendship with Michael is born, and when your family sends an assassin months later to show their displeasure over your failing in the tournament, it's Michael who saves your life. They only stop sending assassins years later, when Ruben exits the quarry after serving his time. It's a bit ironic that they could spend so much money on assassins and not on Ruben's sentence.

By the time you free Michael's daughter, Elizabeth, you've accepted him and his daughter as your new family.

The End

It's been a long time since you've found someone you can trust. Although this man seems to be honest and friendly, you don't want to chance it with your life. You shake your head in answer to him as you decide to go it alone. As a Ranger, you're almost always alone. You're used to it.

As soon as the fencing starts, you realize this could be a very short match. Both the big man and the woman pick you as their target, and the only thing that keeps you from being eliminated immediately is the advantage of playing them against each other in the small space of the arena.

You duck around the big man to keep him between you and the woman. This forces the woman to move to the side to get around him as well, and by the time she's moved past his broadsword, you've moved again.

The other man tries to pull their attention, but they apparently don't view him as a challenge because they, for the most part, ignore him as they come at you. Finally, the fourth man gets frustrated with this and eliminates the woman by knocking her completely out of the ring when she's not watching him.

You breathe a small sigh of relief as this takes some of the pressure off of you. The big man comes at you with his heavy broadsword again. You slide to the side to avoid it. Another direct block will probably make you drop your sword as each hit from him numbs your hands and arms all the way up to your elbows.

You time the next swing to move inside the big man's reach after he swings, but you're watching the other man as well and don't quite time it right. You and the big man trip on each other as the third man rushes in. You tangle together and lose your grip on your sword. You roll away without it.

The big man keeps his huge sword and regains his feet just as the other man comes at him. He lifts his broadsword to block, but the little man slips beneath his reach and pulls a knife. In a motion so fast you question at first what happened, he stabs the giant man.

No matter how fast the smaller man moves, however, he can't hide what he just did. There's a moment of shock on his face, like he didn't realize what he was doing until the blood began to seep through the other man's shirt.

"I'm sorry," he says, dropping the knife.

"Disqualified!" shouts the announcer as two men hurry in to drag him from the fencing arena.

You rush to the big man, who is now slumped on his knees, cradling his stomach in an attempt to hold in his blood. Tears stream down his face.

"It's okay," you try to reassure him, "they have doctors here to help anyone who gets hurt."

He looks at you without comprehension and then shakes his head. "I don't care about myself," he says. "I need to free my daughter from the quarry. She stole bread for my birthday. A sentence in the quarry isn't right."

Before you figure out a way to respond, two men lift him to his feet and haul him away to be seen by a doctor.

As you turn to rise, the announcer stands up on the edge of the fencing ring to address the crowd.

"Ladies and Gentlemen, our champion for this year's fencing tournament." He points to you and claps above his head to encourage the crowd to follow suit.

You stare at them in confusion. Belatedly, you bow to the crowd.

***

Later, you line up before the King for your reward, still bewildered that you won. When the King stands before you, asking what you choose as the fencing champion, a moral dilemma rolls through your head.

Your Uncle Ruben's a full-grown man

but he's family. On the other hand, the big man's daughter is young to be working in such a dangerous job. You don't know much about her or her father. There might be more to the story than just a stolen loaf of bread, but you don't have time to find out now.

_____

If you pick Ruben, go to page 217
If you pick the Daughter, go to page 223

Perhaps the King understands the struggle going through your mind because he stands patiently, waiting for your answer.

The crowd stays hushed to hear your words as well, and a part of you wonders if your family's up in those seats watching. Perhaps it's this thought that finally persuades you. The entire purpose of you entering the tournament was to help your uncle get out of the quarry. Now, as you stand within reach of your goal, you can't let your family down.

"Thank you, Sire, for this opportunity," you say to the King. "If it pleases you, may I have the debt against Ruben the Baker cleared?"

The King's lips pull up at the corners but the smile doesn't reach his eyes. "It pleases me," he answers in the formal fashion loud enough for the crowd to hear. "His debt will be cleared."

The steward walking behind him takes a note, and then the King moves on to the next winner in line.

You sigh as the strain of competing settles into your bones and weighs your shoulders into a slump. Now that you've accomplished your goal, all you feel is a desire to return to your forest where it's quiet.

A noise, familiar but at complete odds

with your current location, roars through the coliseum. It's a deep, primal sound of rage and deadly purpose. No human could make such a cry.

The tiredness in your body evaporates as you turn towards the sound. A woman cries out in fear, and the group around you breaks apart in panic. They wash around you in a rush to escape. One of the other contestants steps forward to protect the King, who seems to be frozen in shock.

In moments, you stand alone beside the stunned King and his bodyguard. Ambling toward you on all fours is a beast covered in long white fur and sporting fangs and claws the length of your forearm. In the brief moment you have to consider, you wonder where they found such a large snow troll.

The thought disappears as quickly as it came. You pull your unstrung bow from your shoulder, step through and into it, and string the long bow in one fluid motion.

A quick glance tells you the King's bodyguard has done the same as you. His quiver only holds one arrow and you gather he was part of the archery challenge in the tournament.

The troll's ambling gate swings its head upwards every time it pushes off with its hind legs. The eyes rise and fix on your small group.

Then the front legs crash into the ground and the eyes lower until all you have to aim at is the top of its thick skull.

Experience tells you that the skull is impenetrable with an arrow. The ground shakes with the beast's weight, and the eyes come up with the strength of the hind legs pushing forward.

You draw an arrow from your quiver, pull it back into the bow, and shoot in one motion. The arrow whistles away, and you growl in frustration. Before it even hits, you know it's a miss. The troll, smarter than most give it credit for, saw your shot and lowered its massive head to take the arrow over its ears.

The wooden arrow shatters against that skull with a disheartening crack. The King whimpers and grasps the arm of his bodyguard just as the man takes his own shot. It goes wide of the beast.

Out of arrows, the man draws a dagger from his belt. Against the troll, it's a paltry weapon, and you have to admire the man's courage.

You draw another arrow. The troll's long strides have brought it close enough for you to smell the musk of its fur. There's enough time for one more shot, but definitely not two.

You wait, and release the arrow just before the troll's eyes rise into sight. It sees your shot, but not fast enough to avoid the sharp metal of the arrowhead whistling for its eye.

With a solid thud, the arrow hits home on that tiny target. The troll shudders and misses a step. It keels forward onto its chest and slides directly into the feet of the King's bodyguard. A gust of foul breath escapes its gaping mouth, but it doesn't breathe again.

Silence settles with the dust of the troll's slide.

The King gives a whoop into that stillness, and he starts to clap, raising his hands above his head for all to see his gesture. The crowd joins him and, where there was silence a moment before, there's a deafening cheer from the stands. You turn in amazement, taking in the row upon row of people shouting their approval.

After a time of loud excitement, the King raises his hands for silence. The crowd stills.

"What boon would you ask, brave archer, for saving my life?" he asks you.

"My fellow contestant's daughter forgiven her crime," you say immediately.

The King smiles, and this time, it reaches his eyes. "It shall be done," he agrees.

The End

Perhaps the King understands the struggle going through your mind because he stands patiently, waiting for your answer.

The crowd stays hushed to hear your words as well, and a part of you wonders if your family's up in those seats watching. Perhaps your fellow contestant is watching as well. Considering his wounds, he won't be able to work much to pay his daughter's debt. You stand within reach of your own goal, but your gut tightens at the thought of leaving a young girl in the quarry when you have the chance to help her.

Ruben is a full-grown man, capable of working hard. Plus, your family has several members able to pay toward his debt. You don't know if your fellow contestant has anyone except his daughter. That possibility decides it for you.

"Thank you, Sire, for this opportunity," you say to the King. "If it pleases you, may I have the debt against my fellow contestant's daughter cleared?"

The King's lips pull up at the corners but the smile doesn't reach his eyes. "It pleases me," he answers in the formal fashion loud enough for the crowd to hear. "Her debt will be cleared."

The steward walking behind him takes a

note, and then the King moves on to the next winner in line.

You sigh as the strain of competing settles into your bones and weighs your shoulders into a slump. Before you fully relax, however, there's a cry of anger from within the arena.

You turn with everyone else to see a woman stalking toward the group of winners.

"You picked a stranger over your family!" It's her voice that tells you who's speaking. It's your Aunt Patrice, Ruben's sister. "How dare you pick som—"

You step out of the line of winners to meet her before she reaches the group. Two men dressed in the King's guard also approach her.

But before any of you meet her, there's a chilling noise from behind your aunt. The familiarity of it turns your blood to ice. It's a deep, primal sound of rage and deadly purpose. No human could make such a cry.

You wonder briefly who brought a snow troll into the arena, but then you see the giant, white-furred creature and all other thoughts flee your mind.

"Aunt Patrice, RUN!" you shout.

Your aunt turns at the sound of the first roar. Her body goes completely still as she stares at the troll ambling across the arena. She stands between you and the giant beast. "RUN!"

She doesn't move, frozen in terror.

You race to her, barely reaching her before the troll does. With a shove, you force her away from its grasping claws. This reflex action saves your aunt's life, but it places you in the line of the troll's attack.

Unfortunately, the King's men do not react fast enough to save you. The rest of your story is too gruesome to tell.

The King commissions a statue to be placed in front of the arena, commemorating your selfless sacrifice to save a member of your family. May you rest in peace.

The End

The announcer continues to point at you while his shouted question fades with the general roar of the crowd. The longbow rests against your shoulder.

"Distance," you respond.

"Distance," the announcer repeats for the entire crowd to hear and then he points to the next man.

Your palms sweat as the adrenaline from the first challenge slowly fades. You vaguely hear the other three contestant's choices. Only one chooses Distance with you.

You meet the man's gaze and give him a nod. He holds his own longbow at his side in a loose grip. He tilts his chin in acknowledgement but his eyes stay cold like he feels none of the tension from the challenge. On his jacket is sewn the crimson arrow of the King's personal guard. This man may very well be the King's own sniper.

Your palms sweat even more. If he's who you suspect, he's well known for his ability with a bow.

"Next round starts in ten minutes!" The announcer hollers.

You've nothing to do in that ten minutes. To pass the time, you pull out a piece of jerky and gnaw on it while you wait. As the salty, savory flavor fills your mouth, your stomach growls. You didn't eat breakfast because of your nerves that morning, but now your stomach's telling you about it.

The other archer stands in place as well. He stretches his shoulders and flexes his fingers, and then he picks up his bow and walks over to join you.

You reach into your pocket and hold out another piece of jerky to him. Without a word, he takes it, nods his thanks, and starts gnawing on it.

In unison, you both turn back toward the archery field to watch as people hurry about to set up the next challenge.

Closer to you they haul out several cages with small, furry creatures inside. The creatures skitter about like they're chasing each other. You squint and grunt when you realize you're watching Training rabbits. They're raised to never stop moving. You recognize them from your own archery training in which you had to shoot five of them before progressing to the next stage of training.

Along with the cages, they bring out wooden boxes, hay bales, and logs, all things the rabbits can hide behind or skitter over. This must be part of the Difficulty challenge.

You dismiss those preparations and scan farther afield for the Distance challenge.

A box wagon pulls up near the wall of

the coliseum. When it stops, the wagon continues to rock side to side, sometimes tilting completely off of one set of wheels.

"Something big," the other archer comments.

You grunt agreement. Whatever they have in the box has to be big enough to throw the weight of the wagon. The wagon jolts and rocks onto two wheels again before thudding back into place.

"Something really big," you agree, and wipe your palms on your pants.

A snorting growl comes from the wagon, loud enough for you to hear over 400 yards away with the crowd.

"You've shot a bear or two in your time, haven't you, Ranger?" the man chuckles.

A surprised laugh comes from your throat. "Sure have," you respond, "but that's not a bear."

This time when he glances at you, there's a spark in his eyes, maybe of surprise, maybe excitement. You're not sure. He raises a brow in question.

"Troll," you answer. From the snorting growl, you guess it's a snow troll. Just a few weeks ago you had to track one and kill it because it kept wandering into a small village up north. It proved to be a foul beast that tried to throw a broken tree at you before you shot it through the eye.

You glance at the rabbits. Whoever made up this tournament must not know what they're dealing with.

As you've been talking, those preparing the arena have installed tall fences along the archery wedge to contain the troll. They're heavy fences with lots of iron, probably enough to keep the troll in check, but the rabbits and obstacles for the Difficulty challenge are still within the confines of the fences. Snacks and ammunition for a troll.

"What?" the other archer asks.

The announcer steps into the center of the wedge and starts shouting before you can respond.

"For Distance, our two contestants must put down the beast. Whoever shoots the killing shot wins. The farther out the kill shot, the more points you get against those competing in the Difficulty challenge."

He steps back and the crowd roars, drowning out your shouted warning to the other archer.

They release the latch on the wagon, and the troll throws the door free. It scans its surroundings as it stretches long, white-furred arms. It's a good 400 yards out but it spots you and the rabbits in no time. A husky, delighted chortle huffs out of its throat as it slumps down onto hands and feet and starts running your way in a loping gallop.

It'll be in range in no time.

All thought of winning the tournament leaves you. If this troll isn't put down, and fast, it'll tear the arena apart, maiming and possibly killing anyone in its path.

You need to warn the other archer. The only way to kill a troll like this is to shoot through its eye. Any other shot will only anger it.

You also know the troll will go for the rabbits first. Trolls love rabbits, and they're the closer prey on the arena.

If you warn him to shoot for the eyes, turn to page 233

If you shout, "It'll go for the rabbits," turn to page 239

No matter where the troll goes, the eyes are the way to kill it. The skin and fur over the heart thickens the area to the point that the troll has to be within about a hundred yards before an arrow will penetrate enough to stop it. Anything before that will only anger it more than it already is.

"Shoot for the eyes!" you shout.

The other archer frowns, glances at the troll loping toward the rabbit cages, and nods his agreement as he turns and pulls an arrow. He holds it loosely against the string of his bow while he waits for the troll to come within range.

By running on hands and feet, its head lolls up and down with each stride. The eyes come up as the troll's torso rises. It looks side to side before the eyes disappear as its head falls into another stride.

Three hundred yards and it veers sharply to your left, straight toward the rabbit cages.

You and the other archer raise your bows at the same time. The snap of your strings is lost in the crunch of the first rabbit cage. The troll didn't even stop but stepped on the cage and caught the only rabbit that didn't get squished.

It stops long enough to eat the rabbit in two bites, which timing wise, means your arrows bounce off the top of its head.

You and the other archer grunt in unison, and the troll's head swings up. It swipes at the top of its skull but the arrows bounced off and there's nothing to swipe away.

Almost as though it's shrugging, the troll hops to the next cage and breaks it open in obvious glee.

Your second set of arrows glance off the troll's lowered skull and sink into its shoulder. It bellows and breaks the arrows with a swipe of its arm.

This time the troll doesn't go back to eating rabbits. It takes a moment to look around and spots you.

With a roar, it pitches the next rabbit cage into the air. The wooden box hits the ground not five feet away and explodes into shards of wood. Several pieces fly into your leg.

The troll chortles as you stumble, and it throws one of the hay bales next. You dodge to the right and raise the bow before the troll can pitch something else.

The arrow glances off the side of the beast's head and takes a chunk out of its ear. Blood draws a bright line down the troll's head until it hits its shoulder. The troll hauls back and lobs a log into the air.

You pull the bow and aim as the troll rocks forward with its throw. There's a twang from the other bowman's string at the exact same time as you release your own arrow.

The log thuds into the ground between you both but you're not watching it. You're watching the troll. Arrows blossom from its eyes. It stumbles, thuds to its knees, and falls face forward.

The arena's silent for only a second before erupting into deafening cheers. You and the other archer meet eyes. You're tied. What happens now? You don't get to ask, though, as you're led into part of the coliseum where a surgeon pulls several chunks of wood out of your left leg.

While you're being seen, you miss the Difficulty challenge. Considering the troll ate half the challenge, you're not sure what they came up with to replace the rabbits.

Finally, you're led back into the arena and are brought before the raised platform of the King. You've never been this close to him before. He's older with deep lines running from the corners of his eyes.

The announcer steps forward to address the crowd. "The other two contestants have been disqualified for fighting with each other. Before us we have—"

The King stands and the announcer falls silent.

You bow as he walks to the edge of the

platform.

"Never have I seen such bravery in an archery challenge," he says to you and the other archer. "I will not take away from such heroism by trying to come up with a tiebreaker challenge. I don't believe there is such a challenge. What would you each have as an award for winning this day?"

You hesitate, shocked by his offer.

"My uncle, Sire," you finally say, "has been told to work the quarry for a debt. May I have his release?"

The King stands a bit taller and looks you directly in the eye. "You can ask for anything and this is what you ask? Are you sure?"

Something in his tone makes you hesitate again. Did you ask for too much? Not enough? *You can ask for anything.*

"His freedom and a year's worth of taxes paid for the bakery he owes on, if it please you, Sire," you say with a bow, hoping you read his intention correctly.

He beams. "Fair." And he goes on to ask the other man what he'd like as an award.

You leave after seeing Ruben's released. Your family doesn't acknowledge what you accomplished but you're not really concerned. You've lived for quite some time without their input.

Later, the other archer finds you in the woods and joins you by your small fire. He leans his pack against a nearby tree and then sits, using it as a backrest.

"I'd like to train you," he offers. "To replace me as the King's archer."

You agree and in this, you finally find a family you can be a part of.

The End

Knowing where the troll will go first is a huge advantage and, if the man's the sniper you think he is, he'll know to shoot at the eyes. You shout your warning.

The man acknowledges with a nod and, as soon as the troll is within range, you both start shooting.

At first the troll does go for the rabbits, but the other archer shoots and hits the troll several times over the heart. Perhaps he thinks the troll's too far away yet for an eyeshot, especially since it's moving. The troll's not close enough for the arrows to penetrate the thick fur on the beast's chest, but they do manage to anger him.

He stands tall and bellows his challenge. With a thud that shudders the ground beneath your feet, he charges straight for you both, ignoring the rabbits altogether. He stops only long enough to grab a log on his way before he continues.

Since he's charging you on all fours, you don't have a clear shot of his eyes. You dodge to the side, running as far as you can because you know the troll can change direction in an instant.

The other archer stays put and simply backs up. It's a mistake. The troll backs him up against the fence behind the wedge.

It will kill him. Although you see people running to contain the troll, they won't make it in time.

You aren't trying to win now, you simply want to keep the man from dying. Racing to the rabbits, you tear into one of the cages and grab  hold of two scrawny creatures. One of them tries to bite your hand. With an arrowhead, you kill the rabbits and let them bleed.

The troll stands tall, and you hear its snuffing sound as the smell of the blood reaches it. It roars in delight, pivots in place, and comes after you before anyone can react.

You toss the rabbits and pull the bow up in one smooth motion, but your hands are slick with sweat and blood. Your first shot bounces off the troll's forehead.

You shoot again and the troll stumbles, steps again, and tumbles to the ground not more than five feet from you. The last shot was so close and the angle so sharp in order to hit his eye that the arrow protrudes from the back of the troll's skull.

The crowd screams their appreciation, but their noise blurs in your ears as you slump to the ground in relief.

You're taken into a waiting area for the surgeons to look you over. The other archer's there as well. You both miss the Difficulty challenge.

Somehow, you feel the other challenge isn't nearly as difficult as what you just experienced, but when you're brought back into the arena, they announce one of the other archers as the winner.

Disappointment courses through you, but you stand tall until the ceremony finishes.

It's while you're collecting your gear that the other archer from the Distance challenge finds you.

"Thank you," he says. "You saved my life."

"Suspect you'd have done the same for me," you say back.

He nods, treating your statement as simple fact. "I owe you," he says.

This catches you by surprise but it also makes you realize this man might be able to help Ruben. Being the King's archer, he probably doesn't have enough sway to free Ruben completely, but he might have enough to transfer your uncle into a different line of work to pay off his debt.

You explain the situation to the archer and ask if it's possible to move Ruben to the castle's kitchens. He is a baker, after all.

A small smile pulls up the corners of the archer's lips. "Consider it done."

A few weeks later, you receive a letter from your aunt. It's short and to the point but it tells you Ruben's been moved to the King's kitchens for the remainder of his sentence.

The End

The announcer continues to point at you while his shouted question fades with the general roar of the crowd. The longbow rests against your shoulder.

"Difficulty," you respond.

"Difficulty," the announcer repeats for the entire crowd to hear, and then he points to the next man.

Your palms sweat as the adrenaline from the first challenge slowly fades. You vaguely hear the other three contestants' choices. Two choose Difficulty with you.

You look over at them but neither one looks back.

One, a short man with heavy shoulders, pulls at the hem of his wool jacket. The movement's made to look like he's adjusting the garment but you suspect he's actually drying his palms. The red dye on the hem of the wool tells you he's one of the border guards. Usually such men are tried and true shots because they hold the wall to the north, but this one seems a bit new.

The other man fidgets from one foot to the other while his hands hold his bow in a white-knuckled grip. The grip doesn't seem to indicate fear, but rather a general nervous demeanor. Other than his fidgeting, the man is average height and nondescript in a way you have a hard time pinpointing. He glances at you from the corner of his eye without actually meeting your gaze.

"Next round starts in ten minutes!" The announcer hollers.

You've nothing to do in that ten minutes. To pass the time, you pull out a piece of jerky and gnaw on it while you wait. As the salty, savory flavor fills your mouth, your stomach growls. You didn't eat breakfast because of your nerves that morning, but now your stomach's telling you about it.

The other archers move about. The border guard jumps up and down a few times, still cold from the morning, perhaps. The nondescript man simply continues to fidget like he's got ants on his hands.

You reach in your pocket for another piece of jerky.

"Careful of that one," says a voice behind you.

You jump and turn to find the man who chose Distance instead of Difficulty at your shoulder. He holds his own longbow at his side in a loose grip. On his jacket sleeves is sewn the crimson arrow of the King's personal guard. This man may very well be the King's own sniper.

"Which one?" you ask.

"The shifty one. He likes to cheat."

"Appreciate the heads up," you say and hand over the jerky you were about to eat.

He nods his thanks and heads back to his side of the field.

You watch him go before you turn back toward the archery field to observe the people hurrying about to set up the next challenge.

Closer to you they haul out several cages with small, furry creatures inside. The creatures skitter about like they're chasing each other. You squint and grunt when you realize you're watching Training rabbits. They're raised to never stop moving. You recognize them from your own archery training when you had to shoot five of them before progressing to the next stage of training.

Along with the cages, they bring out boxes, hay bales, and logs, all things the rabbits can hide behind or skitter over.

From the corner of your eye you see a man move to stand beside you. The shifty one, as the sniper warned you.

"This is easy," he scoffs at the preparations. "I should've chosen Distance." He nods farther out to field.

A box wagon pulls up near the wall of the coliseum. When it stops, the wagon continues to rock side-to-side. It jolts and rocks onto two wheels before thudding back into place. A snorting growl comes from inside, loud enough for you to hear over 400 yards away even with the crowd.

"No," you say, "I'll stick with the Difficulty challenge."

The man sneers. "Scared, Ranger?"

You snort. "Nope, just don't want to tangle with a troll today."

He almost responds but his words catch in his throat. "Tr—troll?"

Before you can answer, the announcer steps into the center of the wedge and starts shouting.

"We'll go with Difficulty first," he shouts.

You breathe a sigh of relief. Mixing rabbits with trolls would be a bad idea.

"The challenge is to shoot more rabbits than the other contestants. The farther out or more difficult the shots, the more points you receive. Each contestant's arrows have a different color. We'll tally them up at the end."

He steps back and the crowd roars.

The man beside you begins to step away and you smack his hand.

He drops the arrow he stole from your quiver, gives you a glare, and keeps walking.

They open the rabbit cages and the little, furry savages scatter across the ground. These rabbits aren't cuddly by any means. You let one get too close and they'll chew your pants off.

You start shooting, catching a rabbit before it skitters behind a log, then another one as it comes over the top of a box.

You hesitate as a commotion to your right catches your attention. The shifty man somehow tripped the border guard without the announcer noticing. As the shorter man tries to stand, the other starts taking all the shots that would be near him.

You could keep shooting whatever rabbit comes into your line of sight, or you could start anticipating the man's shots and stealing them from him. It'd be more difficult for you, but it might prevent the shifty man from winning. A last, ill-formed thought occurs to you before you decide on your course of action. If you want to throw the challenge all together, you could cut the man's bowstring, but such a move would disqualify you from the tournament.

If you shoot as usual, flip to page 251
If you steal the man's shots, flip to page 255
If you cut the man's bowstring, flip to page 267

To steal the man's shots, you'd have to slow down and pay as close attention to the cheat as to your own shooting in order to anticipate his targets. Although it'd be satisfying to take the shots from beneath him, it would also probably make you lose.

You continue shooting as usual. You catch one rabbit right before it leaps from the top of a hay bale onto a log, then another one that just darted from behind the log.

You're lining up your next shot when the border guard screams. You look to see him stumble back from the cheat with a knife in his arm.

The cheat holds a hand to his face, where a large welt is starting to disfigure the left side.

"You sneak!" the border guard shouts and swings again at the other man despite the knife in his arm.

The cheat sways backward in time to miss the swinging fist and follows up with a kick to the guard's knee. The smaller man crumples with another scream.

You stop shooting and move in to keep the two men apart. They're beyond reason by now. The border guard swings at you as soon as you're close. He's lost in the haze of pain from his broken leg and stabbed arm and is simply trying to protect himself.

The cheat rushes at the fallen man. You catch him and shove him away.

The announcer catches the man before he gains his balance and, with the help of the fourth archer, subdues him.

You've finally calmed the guard when the vicious rabbits make it to you, attracted by the smell of blood. They bite into your legs with tiny but sharp teeth.

"Gah!" you scream. Kicking your legs, you dislodge several of the little beasts, only to have them skitter back toward you.

It's a few moments before the rabbit trainers arrive with crates to contain them. By then, blood trickles down your legs from multiple bites and you find it difficult to stand. A doctor catches you as you're falling to the ground. He hauls you from the arena and gives you something to dull the pain.

Whatever it is also makes you drowsy. Sleep overtakes you as you watch more men haul in the border guard and the cheat on their own stretchers.

***

You awaken to find the tournament done. By default, the Distance archer won your competition. Disappointment creates a dull ache in your belly, but as you think about the events of the day, you find you're glad you were there to help the border guard.

Beside you in the infirmary, the guard lays asleep. He's not alone, however. A small boy curls against his side and a woman sits in a chair, also slumped in sleep. His family?

Yes, you decide. Being there to help him was worth losing.

You leave the city as soon as the doctor deems you fit. With the extra you earn from hunting trolls in the north, you help pay toward Ruben's debt. It's the best you can do, and you don't lose sleep over losing the tournament.

The End

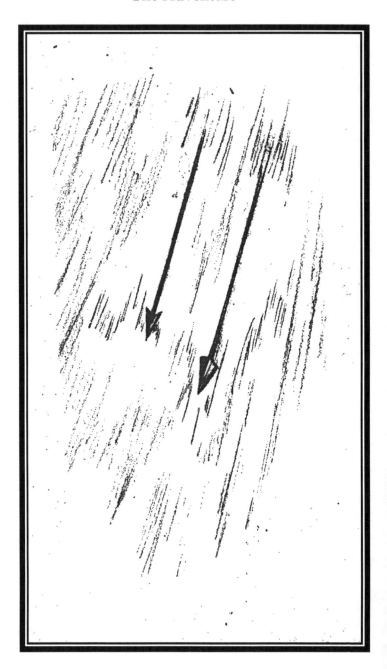

To steal the man's shots, you first must see where he's going to shoot. This slows you down, but when you see the look of consternation on his face after the second and third rabbit that you shoot before him, the slowness becomes worth it. As you're watching for his next move, you see two things.

One is a blur out of the corner of your eye. It's the border guard, who has regained his feet. He's rushing the other man with rage distorting his face.

The second thing is subtler. The other archer isn't aiming at a rabbit. He seems to be picking a shot, but his shifty gaze glances at you out of the corner of his eye instead of at the challenge field. A second before he moves, you're dropping to the ground.

He swings around, raises his bow, and looses an arrow at your head.

At the exact same time, the border guard barrels into his chest, throwing him backward. His shot, instead of zinging by your ears, sails into the air. You track the arrow's trajectory, and your heart lodges tight against your ribs.

The other two archers tussle on the ground, paying no attention to the stray arrow. Others rush toward them to break up the fight, also unaware of the arrow's movement.

All of this you comprehend in a split

second before you roll to your feet, grab an arrow, pull it against the string of your long bow, and shoot.

The twang of your string strikes the air beside your ear, sharp in your heightened senses.

There's a crack followed by stunned silence from those close enough to see the arrow land, and a scream silences the entire coliseum. That scream dies down into relieved sobs from the Queen as she rushes to the King.

Your arrow protrudes from the pole of the pavilion beside his head. Under its heavy head is pinned the stray arrow, deflected from its original flight by a mere inch.

Only now, as you take in the scene, do you start to shake and consider the possible ramifications of your actions. If your own arrow had been off just a hair—. You stop that line of thought before it makes you shake even more. You set the end of your bow against the ground to steady yourself.

"Impressive," the fourth archer, the King's own sniper, says from beside you. "I wouldn't have been fast enough."

***

You realize later how big of a compliment that statement was. The King's sniper is unmatched for skill.

The King, in thanks for his life, frees

Ruben from the mines. He then accepts you into his personal archers to train alongside his sniper. Within the Kingdom, rumors and stories soon develop, talking about the archer's ability to shoot flies from the air and see assassins coming from miles away.

The King allows these stories to fly because it helps protect him and, whenever he hears them, he gives you a knowing wink.

The End

You give the big man's shoulder a squeeze before turning to the announcer.

"May I compete for both of us?" you ask.

The big man gives a surprised grunt. "I can handle—"

A grin spreads across the announcer's face. "NEW CHALLENGE!" he shouts, drowning out the big man's protest. "Follow me, Contestant." He hops down from the corner of the fencing ring and gestures for you to come with him.

A hand grabs your arm. You glance back at the big man. His fingers completely encircle your forearm.

"You better not lose," he says, a dark warning in his tone. "My daughter's life depends on this."

Words don't make it past the lump that's settled into your throat, but you manage a nod before turning to follow the announcer.

He leads you to the center of the coliseum where all of the challenge fields meet like the center of a cut pie. Two men race toward each other on sleek horses in the jousting wedge, and you cringe when their poles smash into splinters.

The archery wedge seems to be in chaos as furry rabbits scamper over bales of hay and wooden boxes. You still can't figure out what's going on in the fifth wedge, but it's to the hand-to-hand wrestling wedge that the announcer finally leads you.

The crowd above this wedge is thin, and no one stands in the chalked circle outlined on the ground.

"Has this challenge not started yet?" you ask.

The announcer grins again. "It just started. Step into the circle, Contestant."

You do as he asks, and two men dressed in the King's guard uniform step into the ring with you.

"This challenge," the announcer addresses the sparse crowd in the stands above, "is not for a prize purse. This challenge is for the chance to join the King's advisors. To get here, the contestant must have chosen something outside of the other challenge options." He turns and gestures at you. "If you subdue these King's men, you will have the ear of the King for the next year."

He raises his hand. Between his fingers hangs a white strip of cloth.

Your stomach clenches. If you can't win a purse, how are you to help your uncle? How are you to help the other contestant's daughter? Have the King's ear? What does that mean?

These questions disappear as soon as the

announcer drops the cloth. You eye the two King's men while you wait for that white shape to touch the ground. They look so much alike that you suspect they're twins. Big ears stick out from under their uniform caps.

Cloth touches dirt and the two guards move, circling the ring in opposite directions to come at you from two sides. Hand-to-hand wrestling is not your forte, but you *are* fast. As the two close on you, you dodge to the left and duck right, behind the man there. In passing, you catch the man's arm and spin him around.

Instantly, you realize this is a mistake. The man moves without resistance. He spins farther than you intend. At the same time, he grasps hold of your shoulders and throws you to the ground.

It's a whirling move that flashes color and people and sky and ground before your eyes in a disorienting wave. Air hisses out between your teeth when you hit the ground. You roll, not waiting to regain your focus, because you're sure the two men won't give you that kind of time.

Sure enough, one man barely misses you with a kick at your stomach. The air from his boot whooshes past. As you regain your feet, you see the other man pulling a dagger from his belt.

This isn't just wrestling, you realize, and you pull your own hunting knife from its sheath at your waist. Your mind races, trying to find an advantage. This entire tournament has been untraditional. Typically there are rules to each challenge, but it occurs to you no rules were stated for this fight besides 'subdue the men.'

The man on the right rushes in, but you see the diversion for what it is. Instead of ducking away, you step closer to him and, at the last moment, push him into the second man's way as you shove his cap down over his eyes.

They both cry out in surprise, and the dagger in the second man's hand slices into his partner's arm.

Before they recover, you see your opening. You grab the bleeding man from behind and press your hunting knife against his neck. They both freeze.

"How subdued do you want them?" you ask the announcer standing outside the chalk circle.

"That will do," the announcer replies.

You release the King's man. He lifts his cap and rubs at his neck as he rejoins his twin across the circle.

"You're now a King's advisor for a year," the announcer says to the small crowd above the wedge to hear. The wrestling match was short lived. It barely drew anyone new to watch. The crowd cheers and then disperses in quiet groups.

You stand in place, confused.

"They're your fellow advisors," the announcer says. "Don't mind their lack of enthusiasm. Come, meet the King."

***

The King's a soft-spoken, older man. Within the first couple days of advising him, you bring your concern over your uncle and your fellow contestant's daughter to his attention.

Nervously, you wait for his response.

"That will be your area of council," he finally answers. "Take a look at the quarry and the workers and advise me on how to improve it."

This isn't exactly freeing those serving time in the quarry, but you soon find you can improve a lot for everyone working there.

"Their food isn't enough," you tell the King once. "For the work they're doing, we're starving them."

The King gives you authority to buy the food needed to feed the workers.

Later, you boldly walk the King through

the tents used to house the workers. Your luck on that day works well since it's raining, and even standing within a tent does not keep the King dry.

"Take a hundred of the guard and build the workers small cabins," the King instructs.

During this time, you keep an eye on the other contestant's daughter and are able to advise for her release a year early due to her hard work and good behavior. The other contestant will probably never know her release was due to your actions, but that doesn't matter.

Uncle Ruben serves his full sentence, but he survives it.

You return to being a Ranger after your year in the King's service. Despite this, however, the King still contacts you from time to time for your thoughts on different matters of the Kingdom.

The End

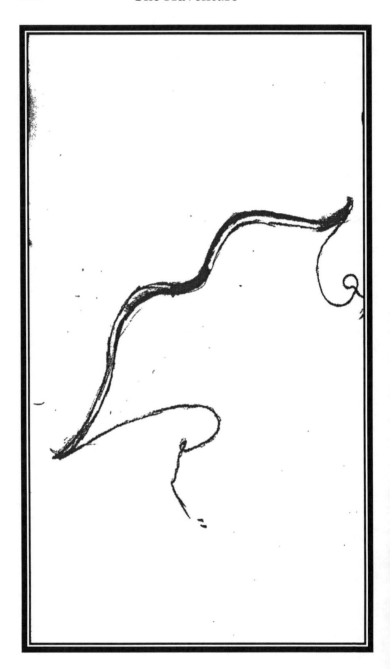

In the moment it takes you to decide your course of action, you realize you probably won't win this challenge anyway. Not because you *can't* win it, but because the border guard looks like he's out for blood now, and you can't continue shooting if he starts a fight.

Before he can rise from the ground, you drop your bow and pull your hunting knife from its sheath at your waist. In three long strides, you move past the downed guard to the shifty man beyond and, in one precise motion, you slice through his bowstring.

The tension on the string snaps with a sharp twang. The wood of the bow rebounds from the sudden release, forward and then back, smacking the man in the face. He gives a small cry and crumples to the dirt.

Stunned silence holds everyone for the matter of a few moments, and then chaos breaks lose. The border guard slumps back to sit in the dirt, staring at the man you just knocked out with his own bow.

The announcer strides toward you from across the archery wedge. From the look on his face, you've just made a terrible mistake.

The crowd above the coliseum shouts in a roar so deafening your ears ring with the noise, and the King stands, staring at you from his spot above the contest. You can't tell from this distance if he's angry.

The announcer reaches you. He grasps your arm in tight fingers.

"Disqualified!" he shouts in a voice that carries over the general roar. Considering the size of the man and the noise of the crowd, it's an impressive bellow.

He hauls you, unresisting, from the archery wedge. Once you're under the walls of the coliseum, the noise lessens to the point that you can hear normal conversation. The announcer doesn't stop, however. He continues to move you along until you're even with the fifth wedge of the tournament, the wedge you couldn't figure out earlier.

Within this wedge, directly against the wall, is a hole in the ground. Without warning, the announcer shoves you into it.

You cry out and tumble to the bottom. It's deep. For a moment, you think you're alone, but then something brushes your arm.

"Get out if you can," the announcer says from the rim of the pit with a contemptuous sneer. As he backs away, a slab of stone slides across the opening above, and soon you're left in total darkness.

"Hello?" you whisper.

There's no answer, but as the silence settles, you pick up on a soft sniffling sound.

"You okay?" you ask.

Sniffle, sniffle. "We're stuck down here." The voice is muffled, like they're spoken against up-drawn knees, but you can tell the speaker is female.

"There's got to be a way out," you encourage.

"I've tried," she answers.

"What have we got to work with?" you ask.

She tells you of her knife and her sword, lamenting about the dirt walls and the stone slab above.

"Maybe we can climb up to the slab," you say. "May I borrow your knife?"

She hesitates, but then the hilt of the knife touches your arm as she passes it. "Don't leave me down here," she says.

"Of course not." You accept the knife. It's an inch shorter than your own with a smooth handle.

You managed to keep your own knife even with the announcer's rough handling. With the blade, you test the dirt and find it soft enough to shove the first few inches of steel into the wall.

You reach as high as you can and shove the second knife in. It grits against the blade but sinks as far as the first. A quick test to see if it holds your weight brings you a glimmer of hope. Being a Ranger has made you strong. The pit's not so deep that you can't haul yourself to the top using the knives as handles. What you do once you reach the stone slab at the top, you're not sure yet, but one step at a time. You haul upward and shove your knife higher into the wall.

"What are you doing?" the girl asks.

"Climbing," you grunt in answer while you pull yourself higher.

You swing your right arm upward. Resistance meets the blade for a moment before it sinks and continues right on through the wall. When you pull the blade back out of the dirt, faint light shows through.

"Look," you say, "light!"

Three more stabs at the wall and you've got a circle the size of your head.

The girl jumps up and down to see through. "Can we fit? Can you dig more?" Her excitement lends its own motivation as you continue.

Your left arm, from which you're hanging, starts to shake with strain. Unable to hold longer, you drop back to the floor to rest.

"One more time," you say. "We're almost there."

The climb back up makes your arms shake and your shoulders burn. Not wanting to hold on for too long, you swing the knife blade in rapid succession until the hole is large enough for your shoulders.

"I'll go through and hang down to pull you up," you tell the girl before entering the hole.

She whimpers. "Don't leave me. Please, don't leave me."

Beyond the pit is a dark hall. No one's about. You turn on your stomach and hang down into the pit, using your legs to brace on the walls.

"Grab my hands," you tell the girl. Her small fingers grasp yours in a tight grip. You haul her small frame up until she can grab the edge of the hole, and then you back out of the way for her to slide through.

Once free, you both sit on the hallway floor, panting and covered in dirt. You grin at each other in triumph.

A lantern lights up the end of the hall, but there's nowhere for you to go. You sit and watch the approach of three men. As they draw near, you scramble to your feet, realizing one of them is the King.

Your stomach sinks but you bow anyway.

"Didn't try to leave you?" the King asks.

"No," the girl answers him. She hasn't moved from her sitting position.

The King turns to you. "Record time in breaking free." He smiles. "Didn't leave your fellow prisoner behind and stopped a cheat in the competition—" he pauses, sizing you up. "Welcome to the King's spies. You've just passed your first test."

***

You find out over the next while that the King uses the tournaments to find new spies. You train with Vivian, your fellow prisoner, for the next three months before you're sent out on your first mission.

It's the first of many. Your family never finds out what happened to you but, being a spy, you have your ways of keeping an eye on them.

Uncle Ruben survives his time in the quarry and returns to being a baker.

You remain the King's spy and work with Vivian for many years. You even get to pick new spies, setting up entry tests for them at the tournaments.

The End

Acknowledgments

How do authors do this? Honestly? There are so many people I need to salute for their hard work on this project. So. Many. People!

First there's my family. One, thank you for your cheering-on when my energy levels flagged. Second, thank you for all the beta reading, voice recording, trailer making, passing out of fliers and much more. You all put in so much more time than I would have anticipated.

Next is Kym O'Connell-Todd for your wonderful editing skills. Your gentle guidance and advice made me believe this book was truly possible.

I can't thank Joseph Apolinar and Justin Allen enough for their amazing artwork. This book has over fifty illustrations and you both put in an incredible amount of time! I absolutely love the artwork that came about as a result.

Thank you to the Bovee's for your sound equipment and audio editing skills, all given spur of the moment.

Thank you to Jaroslav Vyhnička for allowing me to use your Colossal Trailer Music. I'm blessed by your generosity.

Also, there are some who went above and beyond to help me get the word out. Mollie

Bond, David and Susan Leiber, Kaydee Glumac, and Bryan Smith, you all deserve giant hugs!

And lastly, thank you to my husband. You're always there, encouraging me to pursue my dreams and never letting me settle when things seem impossibly difficult. I love you beyond words.

I'm sorry if I missed you here. Thank you to all the Kickstarter backers and people who helped spread the word and anyone else I'm forgetting at the moment.

You're all amazing!

Jennifer M Zeiger grew up in the Rocky Mountains of Colorado. She now lives in Washington with her husband, Nate. The kids include one shepherd/husky mix and two small fur balls of the purring variety.

Note from Jennifer:

Hello Dear Reader. You got to the end of *The Adventure*! I hope that means you enjoyed it. Whether or not you did, thank you for giving of your valuable time. I am truly blessed to have such a fulfilling job, but I only have that job because of people like you. People kind enough to give my books a chance and spend their hard-earned money buying them. For that I am eternally grateful.

If you enjoyed this book and would like to help, then please consider leaving a review on Amazon, Goodreads, or anywhere else where readers visit. The most important part of how well a book sells is how many positive reviews it has, so if you leave one, then you are directly helping me continue on this journey as a fulltime writer. Thanks in advance to anyone who does. It means the world to me.

Feel free to contact me (all details can be found at www.jenniferzeiger.com), as I would love to hear from you.

Made in the USA
Columbia, SC
03 June 2023

17296038R00171